WHEN GOD LET ME SPEAK

When God Let Me Speak

A Short Story Novella

LISAMARIE THOMAS

Lisamarie Publishing LLC

| i |

Copyright © 2021 by Lisamarie Thomas

WHEN GOD LET ME SPEAK

Lisamarie Thomas

WHEN GOD LET ME SPEAK

A Short Story Novella

LISAMARIE THOMAS

Lisamarie Publishing LLC

First Printing, 2021

Table of Contents

Dedication

This Book is Dedicated To

Lianna and Elijah - My Children

Raimundo Thomas - My Dad

Lorraine Coates - My Mom

Lisa Coates - Also My Mom

Loretta Mack - My Nana

Valerie Clemons - My Favorite Aunt

Stephon Thomas - My Baby Brother

Michelle Senior - My Sister

Johnny Thomas - My Step-Father

Kokaine Flo - My Fiancé

Also dedicated to black and brown girls everywhere. It's time for us to realize who we truly are.

Disclaimer

General Content Warning:

The views and opinions expressed in this article are those of the authors' and should be viewed as such.

When God Let Me Speak, is autobiographical, in nature.

All of the stories explain true events however, due to the sensitive nature of the content; some of the characters' names have been changed or altered for their protection.

Explicit Content Warning:

THIS BOOK CONTAINS SOME ADULT LANGUAGE AND CONTENT.

MAY NOT BE SUITABLE FOR ALL READERS.

VIEW AT YOUR DISCRETION.***

Excerpt from Turned Out:

My abuser looked at me with confusion.

As he inflicted pain on me,

I started to thank God out loud.

He didn't know why, but I trusted my God's voice.

My name is Lisa Marie Thomas.

I'm a twenty-three-year-old black woman.

In 2016, I was human trafficked, brutally abused, robbed multiple times, and terrified out of my mind.

I became estranged from my family. I had communication cut off from the outside world, and it changed my life. It ultimately started to change the way I viewed myself.

After living a nightmare for almost a year, I ran away from my abuser. When I survived his last attack in a hotel, I was able to contact my mother, who lived a few hours away.

I thought, "What about Leah?"
Right then, he dropped me, and I fell.
I heard a voice say to me,
"This is the last time."
I knew it was Him;
I knew it was God.

I said,

"Thank You,

Thank You, God,"

because I knew that I could trust him.

I knew He was right.

"In February of 2017, I went back to Clayton County, GA, under the protection of victim witness advocates and a team of support from the District Attorney's office.

The trial was a week long, and my abuser defended himself Pro-Se, under the sole basis that I would not show up to testify against him.

He didn't know that this was about me. This was about my daughter and my life. This was about what he stole from me and so many other women.

This was so I could sleep at night.
On a Thursday,
I testified against him.

He had to cross-examine me, and I had to face him. I knew I had to do it. There were too many lives at stake.

I feel that the reality of sex trafficking needs to be an issue that is discussed more in the African-American community.

Prelude

For those who have not read my first book, allow me to catch you up to speed.

Let me first say welcome to the second part of my story. Turned Out was the foundation of my life, and a short glimpse of my development into this world; to say the least.

For almost a year, I was made to sell my body to dozens of men a day.

I went through stages where I lost my identity, my faith, and at one point, I believed I might have been losing my soul.

After going through circumstance after circumstance, one would think that I had learned my lesson, but I hadn't.

I kept some of the same friends, fell for some of the same lies again, and tortured myself into figuring out who I really was and what I was put here to do.

My first novel, Turned Out,

documents my survival of human trafficking.

To understand some of the characters in the story and their initial role in my life, I highly suggest going back to read my memoir.

What you are about to read in the next story is about my life after the fact.

Many of the experiences that you will journey with me thoroughly shaped my perspective as a woman, daughter, mother, friend, and overall human being.

I truly hope my experiences can help someone else avoid problems in their life or understand what they are going through just a little better.

Everyone needs to know they aren't going through this life or experiences the same shitty things alone.

If no one understands you, I do.

I

Finding Myself

I can never understand why I've always taken the abrupt end of the stick.

I've always been the person to bring people up when they're down.

I've always been the person to understand
when everyone else didn't.

I've always been the person to help people
make it to the top, while they have left me
behind.

1

2~LISAMARIE THOMAS

I've always been the one to bring peace
while constantly fighting my own demons.

I've always tried to be the bigger person and ended up hurt.

I've always been the person who never wanted to give up on people, even when I gave up on myself.

I've always been the type of person who people call strong.

What if I'm tired of always being strong?

What if I'm tired of always doing for others what I can't even do for myself?

Trying to be a good person is not always easy. People will underestimate and misunderstand you.

It's easier to be comforted alone sometimes.

WHEN GOD LET ME SPEAK~3

No one ever wants to have invalidated feelings.

No one ever wants to feel like their feelings are invalidated.

I'm blessed because at least I can say what I need without judgment.

All I have to do is write it down.

There is nobody to counter what I say or make me feel incompetent.

I can get everything out without feeling unheard. There is no one to make assumptions without really knowing who I am.

The journey to finding one's self is long and hard.

I'm unprepared, but I have faith that I will make it.

The stumbling blocks can no longer get in my way because I'm confident in only myself. I'm trusting myself now.

I'm not perfect, but I'm aware of my problems. I just need a little time to fix them. I don't have anyone to pick me up when I fall or let me know I don't have to be strong all the time.

I have to keep going despite the feelings that make me human.

4~LISAMARIE THOMAS

Someone told me I would never find love, and that it wasn't for me.

I thought he was wrong, but maybe he was right.

Maybe that was God telling me I needed to love myself more.

Maybe that was God telling me I needed to

know myself more.

Maybe I needed to listen.

Maybe I just needed a change of perspective in order to realize my purpose.

I don't want to fear anymore; I just want to be happy.

I still don't know what will make me feel complete, but I am grateful to have a voice.

I am grateful that God showed me a way to move forward with my life.

I am grateful for another chance at life.

I am grateful to have a gift, and with that, God Let Me Speak.

1. I

Are You Afraid?

Could you admit you might be afraid to know who you really are?

Most, if not all of us, say that we want to know our purpose in life and who we were born to be. What if you were born to save the world?

Could you honestly say that makes you excited, or does that make you question your ability to handle the challenges?

They say, with substantial power comes great responsibility.

Is that what you really want?

5

6~LISAMARIE THOMAS

I honestly don't know if that's what I really

want. I want a normal life and just to be happy.

I want to live a financially comfortable life, but
the greater calling that attracts me is the same
thing keeping me knee-deep in doubt of myself.
Then I wondered if maybe, all this time,

I have been fighting myself because I don't want to know who I am. I've always been afraid of change, and more often than not, life constantly overwhelms me. I still craved my innocence, and I wanted to go back, not forward.

I wanted to change the past instead of making the future. Maybe this is my problem. I'm actually making this discovery as I'm writing this chapter, and now I don't even know what to say. How about I just say what I feel?

It seems like I haven't been able to find myself because I've been afraid all this time. So, I hung around in the shadows and let my charisma and dry humor be my positive representatives and my depression and anger be the negative representatives in my life.

I allowed those elements to dictate who I was and force me not to become anyone else.

Here's the thing.

WHEN GOD LET ME SPEAK~7

I stand in the shadows of my mind, not because I'm afraid to come forward and move those representatives but because I'm afraid of what happens if I do, and I don't feel fully prepared.

I guess I'm subconsciously choosing not to come forward.

I wonder how long that will last?

I wonder how dark the hole will get, the longer I run from my true purpose and genuine person?

I I I

The Voice of Lucifer

Sometimes, I sit back and wonder.

If I ever wrote a suicide note, what would I say? How could I explain that something affected me greater than living for my own children that I would have taken my own life?

As many times as I've thought about it, the thought still seemed foreign to me.

It might be worth it to give it a little thought.

Let's think about it now.

How would it go?

8

WHEN GOD LET ME SPEAK~9

Dear Family and Friends,

I couldn't take life anymore.

The End.

Or maybe,

Dear Everyone,

I thought I was strong enough to finish the race, but it turns out that I wasn't as strong as everyone thought.

So, I gave up. I'm sorry.

Nah, I don't like that either.

Okay, let me really think about this.

God, I needed you today. I was falling apart.

Instead of calling on you, I let myself break.

I believed you would only give me so much to handle, but I forgot how to have faith.

I depended on everything else to save me but you.

Today, God, I can't save myself, and it might be too late for you to save me.

Is this your plan?

I know that if you allow me to leave, then my time is up.

10~LISAMARIE THOMAS

I don't know if it was today, but I decided I was done today, and I just hope that you don't punish me forever.

Please take care of my children; please walk with them.

Please help them understand I didn't want to hurt them.

Therefore, I left. If I had a second chance, I would do things over again, and I hope that one day I will.

Until then, I'm sorry.

I just didn't want to fight anymore.

I actually think I like that... what did you think?

1. V

Misunderstood

Have you ever contemplated suicide?

Mind if I ask you why?

If someone told you they wanted to commit suicide, how would you respond?

Would you identify with their pain, even if you were unfamiliar with their struggle?

Or would you be quick to judge and condemn?

There's something about feeling misunderstood. It can make people feel a wide range of ways. Would you agree?

11

12~LISAMARIE THOMAS

You might feel vulnerable, emotional, confused, or neglected.

In this world, there are a couple of major elements you need.

Common Sense and Perception.

Common Sense is the easier one to get since most of us have that, right?

Perception, though, is the skill that is key to understanding your common sense. I took a literary class that proved pretty powerful in

my general understanding of perception. The sole purpose of the class was to get the participants to visualize and actualize things through multiple perspectives. For example, we would take a subject like war or healthcare and analyze it through four different brackets.

Historical, Social, Economical, and Scientific.

I actually think this might have been one of the most important classes that I have ever taken in my life because it taught me both directly and indirectly how to be open-minded.

WHEN GOD LET ME SPEAK~13

One of the worst things we can do when we are trying to navigate life is to make ourselves believe the only reality that exists is our own.

It's also pretty counterintuitive to believe that things only operate how we see them.

If you thought you knew everything about me from my last book, we have a lot to uncover. That's where we're going to start.

This time, we will not make this about me. We're going to make it about you, and me, all of us basically.

My plan for this is simple; I'm going to share some different stories with you about me. Some stories may be about others that I may have witnessed.

Through these stories and experiences, we will analyze the power of perception and how it can lead to life or death.

V

Trick Master

I needed someone to listen to this.

I needed someone to hear me.

This is so personal that I wanted no one to hear this. The thing is, I can't let it go.

Just recently, I concluded I might need professional help. So I've developed therapy.

14

WHEN GOD LET ME SPEAK~15

Here's the truth. After I went back to Albany, I got a regular job. I worked some sixteen hours at a time to get by, but I never became content with my circumstances. About a year later, I decided I wanted to go back to Atlanta. I felt I wasn't naive anymore. I decided I was ready to start my life over.

When I made a move, I was almost ready financially. However, I wasn't making enough to cover everything that I needed to move, and my car note was due every two weeks. I knew I had to do something in order to get where I needed to be.

I made a trip to Atlanta to see my dad. While I was there, I contacted a few of my old regulars. I rented a hotel room for a couple of days. I came back to Albany with almost $1,000. I didn't want to hit plays, but I felt like I needed the money. I felt like I could do it alone and be smart.

Let's be clear. I accepted dates again. This time, I was much more selective. Was that stupid?

Most definitely, and I would come to find that out soon enough.

I had been in Atlanta for almost a year. Everything hadn't been perfect, but I was making it. It had just been me, Leah, and Darren.

I had to admit that being back in the city had become pretty nice.

16~LISAMARIE THOMAS

The bullshit started again. It started with Darren moving his boyfriend into the house on us. He had slowly become a terrible friend to me and was even more rude around the house. They made multiple attempts in the most subtle way to get me to leave.

It seemed like the worst type of betrayal, but honestly, at that point, I was still in denial. The way I thought about it, I had to be in denial by believing that he really was my friend.

I was friends with this couple, and they had a daughter. Their daughter had become best friends with my daughter, and they had just sold their house. They had about a week before their new place would be ready. I didn't mind if they stayed for a few days.

I talked about it with Darren and decided that it would be okay. This is where things get complicated. The couple was having a rocky relationship that would end in her and her daughter moving back to New York.

My guy friend stayed at the house for a few more days and then came the next night.

I was about $200 late on the rent in a period of finding a work-at-home position. Leah was at her dad's house for the weekend. I set up a date.

WHEN GOD LET ME SPEAK~17

I figured I could do a quick visit that would put

me exactly where I needed to be. I posted an ad on this new site that I had been using. I hadn't used it much, but from what I heard, it was profitable, exclusive, and safe.

The night went by, and only a few people

reached out to the ad. They seemed nice, and they all stood me up. Finally, someone showed up. It was about three in the morning. Leah was at her dad's for the night, and every-one else was in their rooms sleeping. The only person in the house that was still awake was my guy friend.

I told him what I had set up and asked him to stay up in his room for safety reasons. It was late, so I was a little skeptical, but when I heard the knock, I cautiously answered the door.

This guy was black, in his mid-thirties, and kind of heavy. I was much more skeptical by the time he walked in and sat down on the couch. He just seemed a little too comfortable. He didn't appear or sound the same as he did on the pictures and on the phone.

He asked if he could see what I looked like. I thought he might have been the police, and I might go to jail for solicita-tion.

18~LISAMARIE THOMAS

I was pretty sure that would suck. I pulled my leggings down, just a tad.

Only a single strap of my thong was visible.

I gave a subtle hint about putting the donation down wherever he felt comfortable. That was when he said, "Oh, I got the money..."

Out of his red jacket pocket, he pulled a small 357 with a red beam, right in the center. He propped his leg up slightly and gently laid the small gun on his thigh. Then he said, "Take off your clothes."

My eyes watered, and I gave a minimal amount of hesitation. That was when he repeated himself and cocked the gun back. He stared directly into my eyes with a look of pure evil. A single tear slid down my face, and I took my pants off. A low groaning noise left his throat. I started praying to God that I was going to survive this night.

He asked me who else was in the house. I told him that there were two people, my roommates, and they were a couple sleeping in their room.

WHEN GOD LET ME SPEAK~19

I also told him that one of them had to wake up at 4:30 in the morning for work. I was hoping for two things.

- I hoped he was not there to kill. I knew, if he wasn't, that he would take measures to get out silently.

- I was also hoping that providing a timeframe to when someone would know what was going on would speed up the process.

As he sat on the couch, he looked around. He told me to take off the rest of my clothes. Then, with his gun, he pointed for me to lie down on the couch. He got up and got on top of me. While trying to slide his pants down, I assume he thought he was being too loud. His next move was telling me to go into the kitchen. That slightly confirmed my first thought. He may not have been here to kill. I needed to make sure that things stayed that way.

I had an iPhone sitting on the table in my living room. He picked it up and, with the gun pointed at my head, walked behind me into the kitchen.

20~LISAMARIE THOMAS

He went and stood right in front of

my stove and told me to get on my knees. Then, he shoved the phone in my face and told me to unlock it. I did, and once more, he put the gun on my face and told me again to get on my knees. I knew what was about to happen, and my mind couldn't believe it. Like I thought, he pulled his disgusting penis out of his pants and forced it into my mouth.

With the most force that he could muster, he continuously pushed my head forward and backward until I could feel the vomit sitting in the back of my throat. The vomit came up in my mouth and went back down my throat. I had felt light-headed, and I thought that I might have been losing consciousness until I saw a bright light in my face.

When I looked up, he had my phone in my face again. This time, he was recording me. The tears poured down my face at the shame that I felt. I had never felt so degraded in my life.

Out of nowhere, I felt pain coming from the top of my head.

WHEN GOD LET ME SPEAK~21

He was trying to pull the straight 24" burgundy wig I had

on from off of my head. The clips ripped at my scalp, but I couldn't scream from the pain.

He asked me if I had a condom, thank God. I told him I did, in the drawer behind him. He found the Gold Magnum, along with my purse. My purse held my ID and two of my bank cards. He stared at my ID for a moment, then simply put my purse in his pocket.

Then, my worst fear revealed itself. He told me to bend over. I saw him reach for the condom, but he put it back. He forced himself inside me.

The pain was shocking. I had to cover my mouth from screaming. He had no remorse as he continued to violate me.

I felt as if I was having one of those "life before death moments." My life flashed before my eyes. Then, it was like the future flashed before me, as well. I could see what my future could be and what my future might be. I knew I had to be checking in and out at that moment.

22~LISAMARIE THOMAS

My mind was trying to fight reality. That had to last about ten minutes before he looked at my kitchen table. He told me to "go lay down."

I felt helpless as I walked over to the kitchen table. I kept trying not to look at the gun. I didn't want to look afraid, but there was no other way to be. He told me to move further up on the table and forced himself inside of me once more. Silent tears fell down my face as he continued to violate and degrade me. He continued to record me. Silently, I cried out in shame and embarrassment. I constantly prayed that we would all survive the night. I constantly prayed that this man would get what he came for as soon as possible.

Then, he asked me the most stupid question in the world. "Why are you crying?" As much as my pride wanted to give a sarcastic response, I simply replied, "Because I'm scared."

He asked me, "Why are you scared?"

never taking a pause between the rape and the conversation.

WHEN GOD LET ME SPEAK~23

I didn't directly answer the question. It scared me straight, I'll admit. That question wasn't worth the answer.

I told him I had a daughter. I told him how much I cared about her, and maintaining my life for her was all I cared about. I told him that was the reason he was even there.

He didn't respond; he just continued to rape me.

Suddenly, I felt the worst pain that I had ever experienced in my life. He had shoved his penis right into a forbidden place. It was unmarked territory for me. It was sodomy in the legal definition. It took everything in my power not to scream. I couldn't risk the chance of someone in the house waking up and walking in on what was going on. I knew that if one of us died, that meant that all of us would have to die. It was that simple. I couldn't take that chance.

A slight shriek, however, left my throat involuntarily.

24~LISAMARIE THOMAS

Immediately, I covered my mouth with my hands, and the tears welled up in my eyes. I couldn't see clearly for a few moments. I felt him forcing himself into me again. He had raped me, again. When I opened my eyes, I could only see the disgusting person in front of me.

There were burn marks all over his hands, his arms, and on his belly.

He gave me this deranged smile and asked me, "Do you do cocaine?" I told him no. Not that I hadn't taken drugs or had done cocaine. It was just not my favorite drug, that was all. My answer was no. Next, he asked if I wanted to be his girl.

By this moment, I knew he was psychopathic and sadistic. However, this is my life and three other lives that we are talking about. I said yes. He told me he would come back to see me. As much as I hated hearing those words, they had given me slight relief.

What I heard him say was, "You are going to live tonight," and that had to be God. Then he came. I never felt more relief in my life because the torture was finally over.

WHEN GOD LET ME SPEAK~25

All I had to do was be calm and do what he said, and I could live to move past this.

He came on the floor and made me find a rag in the kitchen. He made me do it slowly, with the gun pointed at me. I looked around until I saw one hanging on the laundry room door handle. He cleaned himself with it and then threw it at me. I caught it, and he told me to turn on the scalding water in the sink. He made me clean and urged me to clean it very good. Of course, I tried to look like I was cleaning well, but I was doing my best not to contact my body or the DNA, just in case.

Luckily, he didn't notice. He made me clean the cum off of the floor and then told me to stand back up.

I had a Chromebook, the one that had been used to write, Turned Out. He told me to give that to him, along with the chargers for my phone and laptop. I humbly gave everything to him, knowing that I might have been taking a tremendous loss. I didn't want to choose between that and my life, though.

26~LISAMARIE THOMAS

Then it was almost over. He wrapped my things up in his jacket as he pointed for me to walk to the front door. All he had to do was leave, and then it would be over. I held my breath as I passed through the living room. I prayed to God that no door opened and everyone stayed where they were.

By the grace of God, he finally walked out the door, and it was over.

I locked the door and couldn't move for probably seven or eight minutes. I was naked, and I could barely walk. When reality finally set in, I ran into my guy friend's room. He was sitting up on the bed, waiting for me to finish the date. When he turned around and saw the way I looked, he was livid.

There were two types of lives to live, and one of them doesn't include police interference. That night, though, things were different. He told me to call the police; I had to get a rape kit done. That was for my safety. I think it was that night with us that things would change.

WHEN GOD LET ME SPEAK~27

God had given me faith that I was still

somebody. He was showing me that through everything that I had been through, someone still would care for me. God was about to show me I could still have value. He was teaching me how to accept myself, regardless of the situation. Sitting in the back of that police car, waiting to arrive at the Special Victims Unit, none of those thoughts had crossed my mind.

I was feeling sorry for myself. It took no time for me to

feel worthless. I had built internal strength for over a year, to have it all torn down in one night. I knew I would never be the same.

I wished that I could have killed him. I wished I had been the one holding that gun. I wished I had been the one to take every bit of integrity that he had away from him. I wished I could be the one to make him feel dead inside, like I felt.

I couldn't even imagine another man putting his hands on me again. I felt he had ruined my chances of finding a husband. It felt like he had taken my confidence away.

28~LISAMARIE THOMAS

He had compromised my sexuality and made me confused about who I was. I felt tainted and permanently scarred. More thoughts of taking my own life had crossed my mind.

As much as I wanted to give up, something in my mind couldn't allow this person to win. I couldn't let him take the credit for destroying me. He might as well have killed me for that. I looked over at this man, who was turning out to be one of my best friends, sitting beside me. He held my hand and wiped my tears away. He didn't look at me like the trash I thought I was.

I thought I could move on. I thought I could just snap back into life like nothing had ever happened, but that wasn't true. Something had happened. Until I acknowledged that, I was going to destroy my own life. Every day, I walked around angry.

I walked around, harboring the pain that was left inside of me. My friend and I grew closer, and he showed me he was falling in love with the person outside of the pain.

WHEN GOD LET ME SPEAK~29

It hurt that I couldn't see this person who he was referring to. I felt myself wanting to fall in love with him, but it terrified me. I thought I might not have known what love was anymore. It scared me because I didn't know if I loved myself.

I was becoming a tragic mix of depression and anger. I thought I was hiding it well, but it was easy for others to see and to feel. I constantly felt a mixture of guilt and shame. The shame was easy to understand, but the guilt confused me, and that made me even angrier.

I didn't know why I felt guilty. I knew I did exactly what I had to do to survive. It was something inside of me, though, that blamed me for allowing that to happen and not fighting back, even though I knew where fighting that situation would have gotten me. Am I confusing you yet?

If you are any bit confused by this, just imagine what I am feeling right now. I can't multiply the intensity. I became confused about why someone would want me.

30~LISAMARIE THOMAS

I blamed myself for putting myself in that situation. In my mind, something about this had to be my fault. No matter how many times I hear the opposite, that feeling has lingered in my soul. The feeling makes me feel weak and out of control. That is when I realized that I might have been losing my faith again.

I didn't blame God this time, so I needed someone to point the blame at. Why not me? It wasn't anyone else's fault but mine. For months, I wasn't myself. I hadn't seen myself so angry daily before. I had never had so many nightmares. I had never felt so paranoid. I constantly covered my scars with drugs. I had never felt so dissociated from life.

I had hated myself, and no one around had realized it. It wasn't their fault that I said that everything was okay. It wasn't their fault that I said that I had moved on. My friend had become my man. He was showing me I could love as much as it could hurt me. He was constantly telling me I was more than I thought.

WHEN GOD LET ME SPEAK~31

However, as quickly as he was falling more in love with me, I had pushed him away.

It wasn't because I didn't love him. I was just scared that I would never be me anymore. I thought that something that I needed inside of me wasn't there. I didn't want someone that I loved to suffer. It wasn't fair that he would have to suffer because I was suffering.

I felt like a terrible parent again because of my anger. My best friend left a few days after the rape. He said that he didn't feel safe. He had taken all the rent money and left my daughter and me to be evicted. I didn't feel like I had anything else to give anyone.

I couldn't count the number of arguments that my boyfriend and I had. His name was Flo. I couldn't even count the number of arguments that I had started. I always felt attacked, belittled, shaded, picked on, and any other words that you could use to describe it. That night seemed to take my validity away. I felt I had no voice, no substance, and no purpose.

32~LISAMARIE THOMAS

Those feelings had deflected into my relationship and into my parenting. Although Flo and I went through the things that we did, he tried to understand what I was feeling; he tried not to take it personal. Leah did not know what had happened to me, but she knew I was hurting. Although I never directly took it out on her, she could tell that I wasn't the mommy that she was used to. She knew that something in me had changed. They both did their best to restore me. They saw me dying, on the inside, even when I smiled.

It became apparent, now, more than ever, that God had placed angels in my life to protect me. I had watched him create a relationship out of tragedy and faith, and he was showing up how to carry each other. God had used my man and my daughter to bring me back to Him, to bring me closer to Him.

I realized this, then months later, I had gone backward. The detective from Dekalb County, SVU, showed up at my door.

WHEN GOD LET ME SPEAK~33

They informed me they had no leads. They asked me questions about any information that I may have on my assailant, but I didn't have a suitable method of communication. They told me they would put my case in inactive status. The GBI was going to pick the case up and run the rape kit. In my mind, all I heard them say was, "Congratulations, you're fucked."

That was it. I felt like I couldn't take it anymore. I had put my faith in the justice system, and they had let me down. They were just doing their jobs; I know that now, but it never stopped the flashbacks. It never helped me come back after drowning in my sorrow.

All I felt was an empty void. I had never shown so much anger. Everything was being thrown, from chairs to slushes, to screen doors. I needed to get it out. I needed to release what was hurting me.

Flo and I argued for hours, as I screamed about every person who had ever wronged me. We continued to argue until he realized I was hurting.

34~LISAMARIE THOMAS

The floor was slippery from all the slush ice. As he was trying to refrain me and begged me to stop screaming and yelling, I basically collapsed onto the floor, dragging him down with me. We lay there, on the sticky floor, as I was crying and shaking hysterically. His normally aggressive demeanor was no longer there. He held me in the most loving way I've ever felt. He held me and told me he understood and that my feelings were valid. I needed to hear that more than anything.

I heard God speaking through him as we lay there on the floor. As he wiped my tears away again, he told me I had to let it go for me. He told me he didn't want to see me destroy myself. He told me I wasn't the type of person to roll over and die. He told me that Leah needed me. She needed me to be everything that I could be so that she would never have to experience anything close to this.

He told me I had to give this to God and have faith in him.

WHEN GOD LET ME SPEAK~35

He told me to have faith in my purpose. He told me that this was my testimony. That was the day he asked me to be his wife.

It wasn't at that moment, but later on that day. I felt the confirmation. I knew I had to accept the things that I could not change. I knew I had to keep my faith, no matter what happened. I knew I would only defeat myself by giving up.

I had to let this go, however possible, so that I didn't lose myself. I had to continue to believe in God. That is why I decided to write this chapter. So that I know what happened and how I felt.

This is my way of letting it go.

1. I

Toss The Halo

There was a time when I was a kid that I felt like my life was crashing all around me. I was slowly realizing that all the kids at school had their mom, and I didn't. I was old enough to know how blessed I was, but that didn't stop the empty pit in my stomach and all the wandering thoughts.

There was this black-and-white picture that my aunt, whom I had called Mommy Lorraine since I was a child, would keep on the entertainment center in the living area.

36

WHEN GOD LET ME SPEAK~37

It was a picture of my mom in her twenties. A modeling photo, when she was clean, sober, child-less, and in her prime. There were so many thoughts that I had. Almost every time I walked past the picture and saw her beautiful face smiling at me, the most beautiful face.

I always wondered, "What happened?"

It just made little sense that someone with such a bright

future could not sustain it. It made little sense that something could have happened to her that was so horrible that she couldn't take care of my little brothers and me. So, I had to know.

Although it was on my mind a lot, going through school, it didn't affect me as much until my pre-teen years. Just after turning twelve. I do not know what it was about, but there was something about that year that impacted many parts of my life. I was in a very weird stage in life, and I was carrying some baggage that my family would soon come to find out about.

38~LISAMARIE THOMAS

It started when I was eight. One day, during the days where my mother was trying to clean up her drug habit, she had just had my youngest brother and moved into an apartment. She seemed stable enough. So, she could visit with me. I would come over and spend time with her, and I could get just a taste of what it was like to spend time with the person responsible for bringing you into this world.

Even as a young child, I remember feelings of being incomplete. I kind of felt guilty for that because I loved my Mommy Lorraine, almost more than anyone else. I knew she handled my well-being and made me feel loved and guided every day. It was just that I had craved to have some kind of relationship with my mother for so long.

I just wanted to know her.

Then my feelings changed into emotions that I could not describe.

WHEN GOD LET ME SPEAK~39

One day, when she ran to the corner store, her boyfriend

came into my room. I'll never forget, I had on this Barbie outfit. It was white, pink, and green, a skirt-set. He put his scaly hands on my body, and I felt disgusted. There were shorts up under my skirt, and then I tried to squirm away as he attempted to put his hand up my skirt and into my little panties.

The next thing I know, he's covering my mouth with his hands and telling me to "shut up." Then he said, "You better shut up. I'll kill you if you say anything, you and your mom." I was a kid, so I definitely believed him, considering the position he already had me in. Then he tried to push himself inside me, but it wouldn't go.

It hurt terribly, and I practically could jump away from him, but he held my arms down and tried again. I felt pain and screamed although his hand was on my mouth, and he jumped up and left. I guess he didn't find it useful to try anymore.

40~LISAMARIE THOMAS

I just lay there for a minute, and when I tried to get up, it hurt like hell.

There was blood on my skirt, I had noticed. Not a lot, but enough to notice. I looked in my closet and grabbed another outfit to change into. I found another set of panties and threw the tainted clothes in a corner inside the closet. I could hear the faint cry of my baby brother in his crib coming from the living room, and the monster was still in the house. I was afraid to sleep, but I didn't want to be awake, so I took a nap.

That day really did something to me. I had no trust. I didn't trust my mom to protect me anymore, and I didn't know how to feel about men. My dad wasn't around, and my Mommy Lorraine was a lesbian.

My Aunty Val was always around us, and she was a powerful woman. She had been in the military for years, so she never really had a man around. In our family, there were a lot of boy children and a few girls, but the people raising us were mainly women.

WHEN GOD LET ME SPEAK~41

Going through life, that memory faded until I was twelve. I had a lot of feelings of insecurity and understanding. When we're children, sometimes we feel like we would be better if we understood what was going on, but it is true when they say that "ignorance is bliss."

My body was changing, I was having a cycle and hormones, and most of all, I felt like I was less than everyone else. Not only was I adopted, but I was also poor, my mom was strict on us, and we had to go to church three times a week; I hated that the most.

I felt like my opportunities to be happy were limited because of my circumstances.

My mom Lorraine didn't go without her own troubles. She attended Narcotics and Anonymous Meetings, and we would go with her a couple of times a week. Those were actually really fun. They would always have a coffee pot, and all the kids would get cups of coffee with extra sugar and play outside for an hour. If the facility was big enough, we would explore and run through the places playing hide-and-seek or tag.

42~LISAMARIE THOMAS

My brothers and I made a lot of good friends there, and some of my Mommy Lorraine's best friends attended the meetings as well. In fact, one of her friends, Debbie, was having a hard time and asked if her grandson could come live with us for a while. Mommy Lorraine obviously said yes, and that had to be God-decided.

Malcolm and I were already friends, and he was a few years older than me. He was like a brother. We had so many adventures together, and we shared everything with each other about how we felt about life. We both agreed that it was harder than we thought, and that it was sucking.

I was talking to this boy at my church, and he always wanted to play behind the building. We would all play. Malcolm lived with us, so he was there as well. Then one day, this little boy and I were back there alone, and he tried to kiss me.

Then the worst thing happened.

WHEN GOD LET ME SPEAK~43

The memories that I had internalized had come back full force.

I remembered the scaly hand.

I remembered my tears.

I remembered the outfit, and I remembered the blood.

I ran from behind the building and back into the church to sit with Mommy Lorraine; I sat through the whole service, which was unusual for me, and then went straight to my room once I got home. Then, I heard a light knock on my door. I said, "Come in," and Malcolm peeked his head in to ask me if I was okay. He told me I could come to talk if I needed to and closed the door back.

I lay there for a little while and cried myself to sleep.

We could consider my Mommy Lorraine strict. She was on us about our grades. We had to be in before the street-lights came on, and we couldn't stay over at friends' houses.

44~LISAMARIE THOMAS

We couldn't even watch certain things on television, like Cartoon Network, Power Rangers, or BET. If we weren't doing what we were told, she was not afraid to dish out an ass-whopping.

I knew exactly why discipline was important, even at twelve years old. I just didn't think it was always necessary, and I just felt misunderstood. I know that my Mommy Lorraine had great intentions, the best. Growing up, though, I wondered if she understood everything in my head because we didn't share the same genetics. I thought, still, that maybe if my mom was around, she would "get me" more. Sometimes, I couldn't help but feel out of place, and my only other immediate family member there was my youngest brother, Stephon. He was only six.

I knew I wasn't alone, and I knew other people could be way worse. But even so, somehow, I felt alone, and I felt scared of what the world would offer me.

One day, after a bad day at school, I went home and had an entire house to clean with my brothers.

WHEN GOD LET ME SPEAK~45

They hadn't made it home yet, and my Mommy Lorraine wasn't due to be home for another three hours. She worked an hour away, but it was a prominent position, as an Assistant Manager at a Days Inn.

Her job took care of us. That's just what it was, though I was feeling like a burden, like my complete life was a burden. The only thing that I believed I was good at was school, and the kids there didn't even like me. I felt like I wasn't good enough to belong anywhere and to receive the love that other people had. I honestly didn't think anyone would miss me.

That was the first time I ever tried to take my own life.

I didn't know how I was going to do it, and it scared me shitless, but I think I might have been more afraid of who I was going to become. I walked into the kitchen, still thinking that no one was home. I grabbed a knife and placed it on my wrist, gently for the first time. I just wanted to see if I would feel anything.

46~LISAMARIE THOMAS

I didn't know how long it was going to take or how much pain I would be in, but I slowly guided the knife across my wrist.

Malcolm walked right into the room at that moment. He calmly asked me, "What are you doing? Why are you doing that?" I just looked at him, dropped the knife, and cried. He just gave me a hug and allowed me to cry, and I really needed it.

We had a long discussion about life and how important it was. He told me about his insecurities and how he had thought about taking his own life.

Yet he was still here, so that meant that I could survive. Hopefully, one more day. I remember him telling me that things don't always stay the same. That was powerful. It made me think it was possible that I wouldn't always feel that way.

That was enough to change the way I felt at that moment.

WHEN GOD LET ME SPEAK~47

VII

Chamber of Secrets

Things changed the summer of the seventh-grade year. Things changed a lot. I had a new best friend; her name was Sky. I discovered my sexuality a little. I can definitely say that Sky helped me to enter that realm of life. We were both kinda shy, but something about that made both of us a little more outgoing.

It was going into the eighth grade, and I was filling out a little more. Sky discovered she might like girls and wanted to see. One night, she stayed the

WHEN GOD LET ME SPEAK~49

night at my house, and we were lying in my bed watching TV. Next thing you know, she touched me, and I actually liked it. The feeling was soft and almost nurturing.

I started for the first time to feel like I wanted something sexual. I felt this feeling in my body that I had never felt before. I felt like I liked her. I couldn't comprehend everything that was going through my mind. It was something about her that made me want to find out.

She touched me in ways that I didn't know I could touch myself. Everything she did felt good to me, and I didn't want it to stop.

She kissed me, and I kissed her back. That was my very first kiss with her. She made me shiver, and she kept going. She kissed almost every part of my body, and it surprised me she knew what she was doing.

Every time we would be alone, she would shower me with affection and intimacy, and I looked forward to it.

50~LISAMARIE THOMAS

The amazing thing is that we stayed such close friends. It seemed like I had insecurities she didn't and she housed insecurities I was too ashamed to admit. We were the perfect match for each other.

We both had dysfunctional families, so we shared a lot in common. We seemed to make humor out of life, and that was refreshing. Sky was also the first person who taught me about doing music. She had music and poems written to melodies she had made up in her own head. It was amazing. I had just been singing, but I loved to write poetry.

At that moment in life, I became an actual person. I wasn't a person defined by my peers or my teachers. My friends did not define me, or my birth mom. My siblings, or my Mommy Lorraine, did not define me now. I was making my own choices with my body and mind. That was really important to me. Being with Sky made me feel happy. I even felt more confident. I felt wanted in this weird way.

WHEN GOD LET ME SPEAK~51

We talked to guys, and that was fun. We would go to skating rink parties together, and older guys would try to talk to us sometimes. That made us even more confident.

There was something about the secrecy of our relationship that made it rewarding.

Eventually, our sexual encounters graduated. Instead of us exploring each other, we had sex with guys together. We hadn't tried a threesome or anything, but neither one of us was really comfortable having sex with someone alone. We did that for a while, and it was fun. We partnered with the same two guys for a while, and we dated those guys. Their names were Jonathan and Jamal.

Jonathan and I became pretty steady. He went to the local high school, Albany High. He was only a few years older than me and in the eleventh grade. He was actually a proper gentleman, and I liked him a lot. Jamal was a boy thot. He was in the twelfth grade

52~LISAMARIE THOMAS

and hopping from one girl to the next. He tried to keep it on the low because he actually had feelings for her, but we all knew.

The relationship between both me and Johnathan and Sky and Jamal went on for about the same time. Age caused me and Johnathan to drift apart. Rumors and distrust destroyed everything that Sky and Jamal had. Sky had fallen in love with Jamal, regardless of his infidelity, and it seemed like Jamal has equally fallen in love with the insecurity that caused Sky to fall so low.

I noticed that the increasing confidence that Sky had built was being diminished day by day, and that wasn't the plan. It seemed like Jamal had gotten her confidence until we heard the worst rumor.

We were told that Jamal had AIDS.

When Sky called me, it sounded like she would die right then. I honestly thought she was pregnant.

WHEN GOD LET ME SPEAK~53

When she told me, I practically dropped the

phone. I didn't know what to do or what to say. I think I might have prayed, and I know I felt a silent tear drop.

I also knew what she was trying to ask me, so I asked her. We agreed we were going to use protection. So, I had to know. "Sky, did y'all wear a condom? I know that's a dumb question, but I'm just asking…" She interrupted me and said, "Last time, we didn't have one." I tried not to panic. Her mom asked her recently about birth control. I suggested she ask her mom to take her. Then, she could ask the doctor to test her for everything. The next week, her mom took her to the health department. For the next couple of weeks, neither one of us was sexually active. We spent a lot of time studying, watching MTV, and writing poetry and music. We did anything to take our minds off the future. We just wanted to stay in our little bubble. For the first time, I had experienced the possibility of death through someone else's eyes.

Based on a decision that she made.

I can't imagine the emotions that she went through as she waited. Her mom didn't know that she took the test. What if it came back positive?

54~LISAMARIE THOMAS

Her entire life would change, and she wouldn't even know if she would have a future. What if she would have killed herself based on uncertainty? Instead of giving life a chance, she would have never known what God had in store for her.

Her test came back negative. Thank God.

We never found out the status of Jamal.

However, for Sky, she lived another day. Another day at full health and potential. She made another decision and a better one.

She was still in the game, and we are still friends to this day.

VIII

Picadilly's

My dad and I have always been extremely close. Even though he didn't raise me, somehow, I never worried or wondered where he was. Something always told me, even as a child, that my dad was thinking about me and that he loved me. I always found that interesting.

I know what you're thinking, and I'm not crazy. I know something connects everyone to their parents, but not everyone feels connected to them.

55

56~LISAMARIE THOMAS
Some parents desperately want their children to
have that connection with them, and that never happens.

Throughout my childhood, my dad would come down to visit me when he could. There were a few times we visited him when he lived in Atlanta. I was around nine, and my dad called. He told my Mommy Lorraine that he was living in Riverdale and would help her with the transportation costs if she could bring me down to see him.

I'll never forget the ecstatic feeling that I felt when she told me that. I mean, I basically idolized this man and did not know why. I was excited the whole way there and even more once we got there. His house was being renovated, so he paid for our hotel room while we were visiting. Once we got there, we went to the hotel until the next morning.

The first day, I almost jumped out of bed. He came by our hotel room to pick up me, my little brothers, Rodney and Stephon and my Mommy Lorraine. He took us all to my favorite restaurant, Denny's.

Atlanta seemed so much bigger than Albany.

WHEN GOD LET ME SPEAK~57

There were more buildings, more cars, and more people. It was louder and cooler. I thought to myself that, "I might want to move here one day." We ended up having the greatest time with my dad.

He took us to the movies, Dave & Buster's, and different restaurants. He let me know how much he loved me every chance he could. My dad was the only man who made me feel 100% safe. I always knew that I could trust him with every piece of my life, and that never changed to this day.

However, my dad does not know that on the third day of our visit, he almost lost his youngest daughter. That morning, all of us woke up from our hotel pretty early. My dad had a business meeting and would be at our hotel around 11 AM. I remember my Mommy Lorraine asking us what we wanted to have for breakfast. We had become fond of trying all the unknown places in Atlanta that we never got to experience in Albany. So, we decided on Piccadilly's.

We had passed this restaurant before heading back to the hotel the night before and remembered the sign about the breakfast buffet.

58~LISAMARIE THOMAS

We figured it was an excellent choice. It was also within walking distance. It was probably a

five-minute walk, at the longest. We headed to Piccadilly's around 9:30 and headed back to the hotel around 10:15. Now, if you know Atlanta, you might be familiar with where we were. We were coming right off of Old National Highway, and we were turning onto Godby Road.

We were walking and talking. Everyone was in a great mood, but it's funny how fast a second goes by. There's this thing that people say, "It's like I saw that happening before it happened." Or maybe, they felt like they saw it, as it was happening. Maybe they just couldn't react fast enough.

Either way, I never realized this was true until this day. Equally, I never understood how powerful fear was. As we were walking down the street, my brothers and I were holding hands on the sidewalk.

We were still talking, probably about cartoons or something super childish, I suppose. My Mommy Lorraine was just a few steps ahead of us.

WHEN GOD LET ME SPEAK~59

I remember glancing up and noticing her make eye contact with me briefly. Her face had changed a little, but she didn't seem as excited. When I looked up again, her face seemed scared, and I just heard her call my name. She was standing next to me, but she sounded so far away.

She had seen something, and she was trying to tell me, but it was too late. She knew something was going to happen, but she didn't know what. She tried to stop it, but everything happened too fast. I looked down at the ground as I was walking.

Right before, I made eye contact with my mom, as she was calling my name. I looked down.

I saw some kind of animal. It was big and furry. I was afraid of almost every animal created. There was blood, and I was afraid of blood. The animal was dead, and I was afraid of death. My logic went out the window, and before I knew what the animal was, I let out a loud scream that would have woken up the entire City of College Park.

Then in a split second, I ran backward into the road.

60~LISAMARIE THOMAS

The red Honda was coming around the corner. He was flying fast. My brothers immediately held each other in shock. My mom ran into the road after me. I don't even think that the driver noticed me until the very last minute.

My hands covered my ears as I waited to find out what had happened to me. As he stopped, the driver and I made eye contact. I had stopped in the middle of the road in shock, and I felt the wind on my shirt and the warm metal of the car. It was just slightly against my leg. My Mommy Lorraine was about two feet in front of me. She almost got slammed by the car herself, but she didn't. In fact, we were all okay. She stood frozen in fear as my fate waited to be uncovered.

All we had to do was open our eyes. Amazingly, when we did, we found we were all alive. I couldn't believe that I was alive. My brain wasn't even big enough to comprehend the opportunity I had just got, but there was something that I might have to let go of.

WHEN GOD LET ME SPEAK~61

As a child, and even as an adult, one of my biggest weaknesses was fear. I was afraid of almost everything. If you've read Turned Out, there's a lengthy list of all my fears, and to this day, I still battle with navigating and living my life in fear.

Fear is something almost spiritual or energetic that can cause a person to lose control of themselves instantly. It can cause someone to react faster than they can actually think about what they're afraid of. It can also cause a person to be paranoid, constantly thinking, searching, or anxious.

Admit, that's unlike anger or sadness. Even when you're angry, there's a thought that can process. An angry thought has to process at least halfway before a person has a reaction. If not, how would they know what they were angry at? All of us are just living life the best way that we can, but none of us were born knowing what to do.

That means that fear is just a natural reaction to unfamiliarity or uncertainty.

62~LISAMARIE THOMAS

Not only can fear stop a person from surviving, but it can also stop someone from being successful. It's one of the few traits that can control a person's life. Fear is almost worse than addiction.

If you want to follow me a little deeper, fear is probably the number one underlying cause of addiction and many, if not all, of the psychiatric and social disorders there are. It might even be the underlying cause of anger. It's a combination of our genetics, life experience, and external advice or support that determines how we individually react to fear. However, it is the pattern of our reactions to fear that determines our learned behavior.

So, at that moment, my self had almost defeated me. My fear had dominated every part of my body. One element had impaled my logic, my perception, my common sense, and my physical movement. That had almost shut down my ability to survive.

WHEN GOD LET ME SPEAK~63

I should have learned then, but I would learn later in life

how important it was to acknowledge and control the fear in yourself.

1. X

The Messengers

If this was an Instagram story or some kind of blog, you would have known I had taken a break. The last few months have been a roller coaster, and I had a bit of a writer's block. Even though I've been a little under the weather, I've had some thoughts that made things clear and brought me back here to you guys.

It's literally 2:06 AM, and my light-bulb finally clicked on. We talked about how God works through you and me, but this chapter is going to focus on how God works through other people for you and how the Devil does too.

64

WHEN GOD LET ME SPEAK~65

The first time I ever noticed that God was talking to me through a person was during my first pregnancy. I was with my daughter's father, in a Pilot gas station, at about three in the morning. I was ordering a footlong, and there was a Caucasian man standing right behind me. He said nothing, but he seemed friendly.

It wasn't until I poured my soda that I noticed that this man was standing right next to me. It didn't creep me out or anything, but I was wondering if maybe he knew me or something. As I walked off, he finally spoke to me. He said,

"You're going to have a son, and he's going to be something great." Something about this man was different. I couldn't put my finger on it. His intensity had gotten stronger in a glance. Although I felt as if he was talking to me, I felt he wasn't the one talking to me.

I knew I was having a daughter. I can't honestly say that I thought he was lying, but I thought maybe he was kind of inaccurate. It turns out, though, that he wasn't lying, and I had a son, exactly two years and ten days later, on Halloween night.

66~LISAMARIE THOMAS

The next time, I faced the Devil himself. The story of Boss and me was the foundation of Turned Out. However, there were a lot of things that I did not explain. Boss had an intense glare, but there were some times that I saw something else, or someone else, in his eyes.

It was scary because I saw the void in his eyes. I could tell when his soul would leave. It was even more terrifying not knowing who the entity was terrorizing me inside this man's body.

I believed that he, himself, was pure evil, but I also knew that there was an entity that was feeding on my life and attempting to destroy me.

That experience helped me to understand that spirituality is manifested many times through people. As humans, God can use us as a vessel. Sometimes, people are used to bless people and sometimes to curse them.

I'm convinced of that fact simply because everything happens for a reason. Everything comes from God, and there is always a purpose. Even if He only means for us to learn a lesson.

God knows what we all can handle, individually. He knows what we can stand to do, hear, or even tolerate.

WHEN GOD LET ME SPEAK~67

God knows our breaking points, and He knows when we need to hear a word of encouragement.

There are so many people that had positive and negative influences in my life. It wasn't until this point in my life that I finally realized that people are in your life for a reason. It may be the random lady in the gas station that tells you that everything will be okay, and you do not know why she spoke to you. It could be a best friend that you have differences with.

In the short time I've been alive, I've heard so many people tell me things that were not only untrue but also hurt my feelings. Many times, the people I thought would be closest to me said those things. In all honesty, hearing hurtful things made me depressed for a long time. Everything from I'm a negligent parent to being called stupid and lazy. I've even been told that I had no goals.

I got to a point that I was so hurt by all the degradation that I actually believed some of those things.

It wasn't until recently that I had another change of perspective. That took more than a little hindsight, logic, temperance, and realization.

68~LISAMARIE THOMAS

I noticed that every time someone said something to me that devalued my self-worth, I went harder. I worked harder to prove them wrong.

In the most trying time of my life, when I had to deal with the most circumstance and lack of support, I had always overcome. I had used every negative to push forward.

That is the very reason this book was written. I was so angry that I just wanted to have a voice. I wanted to have a voice that didn't just tell a story of tragedy. I wanted people to understand the person who I am and who I am growing into. I realized that one of the best ways to do that was to be honest with myself in every aspect of my life.

I understood through the pain and the shame that this, too, was just a test of faith. Everyone that has ever lifted me up or caused my pain had a purpose. They had a season, and I had to be receptive to the role everyone had to play.

These people, words, and experiences were just messengers in my life.

WHEN GOD LET ME SPEAK~69

At my worst, my four-year-old daughter had been a messenger when she told me that everything would be okay. Just the other day,

at seven and a half years old, she told me,

"Be happy, Mom, and rise."

Just as everyone in my life had completed their objectives, I had to complete mine.

I still have a purpose to fulfill, and every messenger in my life helped me to see that.

X

Red Flag

Hindsight is a beautiful thing. It's much more effective when you've learned to master it. With hindsight comes a lot of warning signs first. Personally, I've always noticed after an incident occurs that there were always things that led up to that incident.

There were always red flags. In my life, I seemed to attract or end up in relationships with men that were controlling or abusive.

70

WHEN GOD LET ME SPEAK~71

However, it was just a few months ago that I realized that I had started and continued a pattern from the time I was thirteen years old, and I had never noticed it.

I started dating this boy named Courtney; it was right after eighth grade. I had become comfortable with my sexuality, and I had become comfortable to have a boyfriend and even having sex. My mom knew Courtney and his family, so she used to let me go over to his house after school sometimes.

Normally his mom would be home when we got there, but he had younger brothers and sisters, so sometimes we would have the house to ourselves. He was a couple of years older than me.

The thing that attracted me to Courtney was his confidence. He felt like he was great, even though he was young. He saw himself in the world. However, I didn't know the difference between controlling, arrogant, or confident, and Courtney had a little of it all.

I should have seen the signs early.

72~LISAMARIE THOMAS

He always had to be on the phone with me. He got extremely jealous over every little thing. It went as far as me having to put him on the speakerphone when I was in the shower.

I started on the dance-line for Albany High in the ninth grade. He went to another high school in the area, but he came to see me every day after my practices and would even show up sometimes. I thought it was cute, of course, but they were warning signs all along.

When we first had sex, things felt natural. Further into the relationship, though, he wanted sex on demand. It felt almost like I was obligated to him because I was his "girlfriend," but in reality, I was just a kid. I shouldn't have even been having sex, but we were both young.

It seemed like we thought that was what love was. It wasn't until I felt a void and out of control that I realized there was something more to life and even relationships.

There was no depth with him.

WHEN GOD LET ME SPEAK~73

Things had become more about him and what he wanted.

That left me feeling empty, even early on. I didn't have any experience knowing how I should treat people and how love would feel, but the relationship between Courtney and me left me feeling wanted but invalidated. There were mixed emotions that would follow me through my adulthood.

These feelings would lead me into some of the most complex and dangerous relationships of my life. However, those same experiences shaped me as a person, so I can't say that I'm completely remorseful or ungrateful. Sometimes, I wish I would have seen the signs earlier.

I could have avoided a lot if I would have heeded the warning that God was giving me. I can say that it has always attracted me to guys that had something street about them.

Some may say that it's because girls grow up to seek guys like their fathers.

74~LISAMARIE THOMAS

It would be a lie to say that my dad wasn't one of the most gangster men I've ever known. To my knowledge.

That could be the problem, but I think my problem might have been bigger than that. I had a tendency to want to help people, and sometimes, a little too much.

When I think about all of my relationships, the common denominator in every situation was that I was giving un-needed help, which was partially because of my tendency to overcompensate.

I based half of that reasoning on me chasing a life I didn't have, and the other half was simply because I was a Virgo.

Either way, neither factor had a positive effect on me. In the mind of the men that I dated, I was trying to "fix" them or "mother" them. In some ways, I guess I was. Can you guess the problem with that?

Ding, ding, ding...

I didn't even know who I was. Through the relationships, I learned how to operate and handle business on my own. That was because I was handling so many things in the rela-tionship. Maybe that was God's way of teaching me that skill, so I'm grateful for that.

WHEN GOD LET ME SPEAK~75

However, there were so many more things that were es-sential to me. I felt I kept losing constantly, and I hated that feeling.

I wanted to inherit things from the relationships, like the money I spent on furniture lost, or moving Leah's dad to Atlanta with me, or his graduation party. I regretted the $3,000 that I gave him from my taxes to get his car fixed because I thought we were a unit. I thought we were going to be together, but things change, and sometimes they're for the better.

I always think back to how much money I would have had. I thought back to the times that I went without. I thought about what if I had a savings account or a college fund for my daughter instead? That's when my thoughts weigh me down.

There's something that I didn't think about, though. Through adversity comes creativity, motivation, and triumph. These relationships had been teaching me to accept life failures and also brought things to my attention that I may not have thought about.

76~LISAMARIE THOMAS

It was the failed relationships and self-doubt that had inspired me to love myself more. They had inspired me to give my children better and to do more investing in myself. Those qualities alone taught me how to maintain, with or without a relationship. Those qualities showed me how to stand on my own.

A lot of the regrets I harbored in my mind. To be completely honest with you, I'm only releasing some of these feelings as I write this. I'm understanding most of this as I'm writing this, as well. So don't feel left behind.

The men that I've dated had anger issues. I thought that was the problem until I realized that I had them too. Most people do.

Could it have been an ego issue? Maybe, but my ego is pretty gigantic, so is my pride.

I thought maybe it was me. Then again, the relationship failures could be a compatibility issue.

WHEN GOD LET ME SPEAK~77

Maybe it was a combination. I think I got my answer.

I was looking for the wrong thing, even in the guys that attracted me. That's why, when I chose guys outside of that character, things still didn't work out. First, I was actively looking for an image. I thought it would be almost impossible for me to have someone that did not attract me. I was also looking for potential.

I felt I knew where I wanted to go in life, and I wanted someone that seemed to match that. I was looking for someone that wanted to be loved instead of looking for someone to love me, as well.

I was looking at dominance in a man as a strength. I didn't realize that vulnerability in a man was equally a strength. It wasn't until I was smack dead in the relationship that I understood that I was building these men up and I was being brought down, whether they intended to.

I went through some mixed emotions, thinking that I was just bad at love. Then again, a light-bulb switched on in my head. Besides the known factors, there was one unconsidered.

78~LISAMARIE THOMAS

I'm sure that you all guessed this one before I did. I was constantly looking.

Let me be clear; I wasn't trolling the internet and grocery stores searching for a man. The thing was, with every guy that showed interest in me, I would see the potential of a relationship. I was still looking for something. That was a major problem.

I had to let a man come to me that was not only strong but also honest, emotional, and vulnerable. I need someone to see the potential in me the same way that I see it in them. I need someone to recognize and merge my fears.

I need someone to understand my psychological pain and be as nurturing to me as I am to them.

I didn't need a man that was shy about how he feels. It took even more time to realize that I justifiably needed to be validated, the same as I would for the person who I loved. I don't need to be coddled.

What I need is patience, tolerance, motivation, security, and growth.

WHEN GOD LET ME SPEAK~79

That's what any solid relationship needs. That's what God provides when he sends someone to you. This is a little exaggerated, but it took for me to be damn near twenty-five with fifty years of emotional, psychological, and physical trauma to be receptive to what God has been trying to show me all of this time.

It's strengthened me, and I believe that gives room for the man that God sends for me to help me gain the peace that I need. I wonder what this man will look like or what kind of person he will be.

Would he be a normal nine-to-five working man, or will he be a thug?

Truthfully, he'll probably come from the streets because he'll understand me, and I'll understand him. This man, although he has an ego, will know how to compromise. The world might wear him down, like me.

He might be angry at the world, but he doesn't want to be. He's going to be smart regardless of his background.

80~LISAMARIE THOMAS

He's going to strengthen me. More so than I thought I was. He's going to show me strength that I never realized I had. He's going to benefit me mutually, as I do him. He's going to be a leader in his own right. He's going to be king-like, and he may not know it. He's going to show me how to acknowledge his mistakes. That will teach me, as well. His character will shine because his morals and mind frame make everything about him.

We'll grow from each other, and he won't be afraid to love me. He won't be afraid to allow me to love him. We'll be not only a reflection of each other, but we will also reflect who we used to be.

Our connection will be spiritual and not based on any religion. It will be because we listened to the calling on our lives that brought us to one another. It will be because we listened to His voice and accepted God's blessing. It will be because we both earned it, and we both deserve it. It will last because we both have been molded and willing to change for each other. We will push each other to be greater, and it won't be forced.

I want that for my life.

WHEN GOD LET ME SPEAK~81

I'm listening to God, and instead of waiting patiently, I'm keeping busy so that I don't miss the bigger picture as well.

With regret, I can never say that I blamed God. I only blamed myself for not making better decisions. However, even that is the wrong way to think about it. If I was going to blame myself for anything, it should be for not listening to God. Then again, that might be the wrong way to think about it too.

I should be grateful that I even noticed the warning signs. My life could have been worse. Instead of constantly thinking that I lost something, lost myself, or even lost time, I could be grateful for the work that God was doing on me.

I could accept that my blessing will come in his time and not mine. I could be more than grateful that God has been preparing me for the right man to come into my life.

82~LISAMARIE THOMAS

I could be thankful that I didn't settle for someone that doesn't complete me.

I think I'm willing to wait on the man that God has for me and for my children.

I think I've had a change of perspective, and I'm grateful for that.

1. I

Non-Denominational

I'm going to start this chapter by addressing the elephant in the room, or the book for this matter. I'm not a Christian. Let's be clear. I believe in God. That should be obvious, right?

However, I was never one to be persuaded by religious concepts. It became apparent to me that religion had a way of dividing people and dividing perception.

Every time I walked into a church, I noticed people had a way of changing people's minds.

83

84~LISAMARIE THOMAS

They could walk in a building, listen to someone talk to them, and immediately feel differently about themselves. Whether they felt better or convicted, there was a pastor, preacher, or the like, giving a sermon, speaking on what is "good and bad" and how people should live their lives.

Ultimately, it was a human that could change how a person viewed themselves.

I grew up in a family where gay was a common sexual preference.

I noticed that the pastors in the church would talk about people that were gay or prostitutes. They would speak on subjects that were "as they considered" not of God.

However, I'm ten years old, sitting in the front pew, thinking to myself.

"How do they know what's not of God?"

Sure, they had a book that gave the "rules" that we had to follow, but that was just a guide. We weren't supposed to judge. So, why did so many churches make people of different orientations feel bad about themselves?

Why do they turn some of them away? Why do such "Godly" people "clique up" to run people they don't like away from their churches?

WHEN GOD LET ME SPEAK~85

Why do women gossip after Bible study? Why didn't the church give to the people so that we could as well? Why do Catholic churches expel mothers that had children out of wedlock while their leaders continue to rape little girls and boys?

Why do we come to church every Sunday to pay for words of encouragement and go back to the same shitty lives with our newly gained mustard seed of faith? None of it makes sense to me.

You've probably wondered why I included this chapter, and that's simple. How I speak about God is clear but in no way, shape, fashion, or form should this be mistaken for some kind of religious novel or self-help book. One of the biggest elements to survival is a person's mind frame.

I meant this chapter to counter religion and everything that it stands for because it has not been religion that has kept me alive and keeps me going every day. It has not been religion that has saved my life many times.

I also understand that religion is a controversial topic. So, allow me to extend further clarification.

86~LISAMARIE THOMAS

This chapter is not to bash religion

or anyone with religious beliefs.

Now, let's continue.

I respect everyone and their views. In this chapter, although countering is a factor, separation is the focus point. Religion and spirituality are two totally different things.

You may say "spirituality" is a man-made word, and I would agree, but the definition of spirituality is

God-sent.

The energy and spirit that makes us human should be the religion that we choose to reflect. It should be a complete love of self and connection to your inner person.

This is where God speaks to you, where He guides you from and reveals your purpose.

Too often, in our cultures, the lines of spirituality and religion are blurred. Spirituality is not something that you have to choose to accept or become bound by. It is the moment that a person's true self is revealed to them.

It is the moment that they realize that their role in life is to fulfill a higher purpose.

WHEN GOD LET ME SPEAK~87

It is the moment that we use the resources given to us, like the Bible, to search for the message that God has for us. That is not something that can be received in a general sermon or under general orders. It becomes the moment that a person can clear their communication channels so that they only hear themselves and God.

One body in one mind. It is at that point, when we all can reach out to God from inside ourselves and know that we are Him, that we can all walk in our purpose. As a people, country, or entire Earth. Our individual orders given by God are what make the plan for a perfect world. A concept that takes something so personal and makes it a general statement may be the reason the world is in dismay.

We are all seeking to be united physically in order to summon God to change what he created. However, we can't expect him to change a blueprint that needed no changes.

Can we?

Can we expect a chair to be put together if we disregard the instructions given and create our own?

88~LISAMARIE THOMAS

We have a chair, sure, but how long will that chair last

and how great could it have been, had we shown more discipline?

For my people, especially my young people,

I know that religion is systematic, and there is no problem with connecting with God AND sticking to your beliefs. I'm just saying that one of the most important things that we can do is acknowledge the divide. We have to become able to separate the concepts of mass religion from who we are and who God made us to be. In that, there is a lot of strength and purpose you may not have known that you had.

Before I found God within myself, religion was the thing that stood in my way. By that, I mean not only did I care about what other people thought about me from a personal standpoint. It got to a point that I felt uncomfortable in a room with Christians or other religious people because I felt like I wasn't living life up to their standards—the standards that would admit me into heaven—and that was scary.

As a young girl going through life, I didn't want to worry about the possibility of going to hell for every wrong thought, action, or mistake. That instilled fear in my heart and mind.

WHEN GOD LET ME SPEAK~89

God didn't create us to be afraid. I believed that the church was standing in my way of realizing who God had made me to be. I felt I was being programmed through religion to live my life, a certain type of way.

I didn't think that it was okay to feel at fault for missing an opportunity to congregate with people that God created equal to me. We were all people, "even by religious standards" is one. Some call it the "Body of Christ."

My question is, "If all that is true, why isn't our power greater? Why doesn't it stretch beyond the walls of any congregation or building? Why aren't we able to unite and move mountains with the other 90% of untapped, God-given potential resting in our minds?

Why would God consider a 10% tithing from a person's wages to be mandatory for the operating expenses of a building?

If we owe 10% tithing to God, and He is within everyone, shouldn't you be tithing back to yourselves and your family?

90~LISAMARIE THOMAS

Before there were church buildings, where did that 10% go?

Did Jesus take it?"

It seems funny, when you think about it, that God gave us the correct formula and solution to our oppression as a "minority" people. One of the most impactful, while living in America, and that was the key to poverty.

This world is not all good, and there are many that realize that the majority are really the minority. It is really us, whom they call the minority, that populate and fill the Earth.

In my eyes, religion is nothing but a way to keep people in a box.

Religion can cause you to be blind, thinking that you can see because you are being led. God gave us people to spread knowledge, wisdom, resources.

He didn't create us to depend on someone else's understanding. We may need to be advised by some, we may need some support, or even motivation from each other, but we don't need to be taught by someone.

We don't have to go through a weekly process or speak on a prayer line for God to hear us because he is us.

WHEN GOD LET ME SPEAK~91

He's constantly sending people into our lives to deliver messages we need along the way; we just have to listen.

Listen to ourselves and realize that we are the God we have been searching for our complete lives. We are our own peace, and everyone else has supporting roles in our story, to help us reach the principal goal.

Even a religious teacher is an adviser. We have to teach ourselves how to identify God in our lives. How to have a natural relationship with him, outside of anyone else.

We believe our thoughts are His and that He knows our journey and destination, so there is no need to fear. That's what I realized, and that's when I broke away from religion and found God living in my mind.

92~LISAMARIE THOMAS

WHEN GOD LET ME SPEAK~93

XII

Annabelle

This is a story that I never saw the beauty of. It took me a while to know how important this story was to my life; it might be one of involuntary sacrifice. To some, this story may seem insignificant, but it may have been one of the most significant.

When I was fifteen, I was living with my biological mom,

and I really wanted a puppy. I did not know why, but I felt I would have some comfort having a personal best friend.

94

WHEN GOD LET ME SPEAK~95

I would have someone that I could take care of, and that would love me unconditionally.

My mom and stepdad Johnny told me they would do the best they could to find me a puppy, but they couldn't guarantee anything. It wasn't the most exciting response, but I was happy with their efforts. The following week, my mom surprised me with a trip to the Humane Society.

She made sure that I knew I wouldn't leave with a puppy, most likely. However, she thought it would be worth it to look at some animals that were being put up for adoption.

We walked through the facility, and there were so many cute animals. Many of them I felt bad for because they looked hurt and sad. I knew that regardless of their past, they have been saved from further tragedy, so that provided some relief, but I really wanted to help them. I had a little soft spot in my heart for all the animals, but it was someone in particular that captured my heart right away.

96~LISAMARIE THOMAS

I looked up and saw this blonde, little shaggy puppy sitting in the corner. She was in a cage right in front of me, but she didn't run up to the cages like all the other dogs. I walked up to the cage because there was just something about this puppy.

When I got there, she really surprised me. The puppy came right up to the cage and jumped up as if she wanted to go with me.

The manager of the Humane Society was surprised as well, and he immediately told me that this dog was very shy. She had just gotten there and had brief interaction with any-one. He also told me that this puppy had been through some trauma and had some adjusting to do. He told my mom and me that she would be ready to adopt in a few weeks. I didn't think that it would cost anything to adopt, so I was ecstatic until he told me that the usual charges were about $200. I knew that my mom and Johnny had little money, so I put the thought off in my head for a while.

There was something about this dog that I could not get out of my mind, and that was kind of weird.

WHEN GOD LET ME SPEAK~97

It was exactly two weeks later that I was coming home from flag-line practice. It was the day before my sixteenth birthday. I walked into the house, and that beautiful, blonde shaggy pup was sitting in our living room. I practically screamed out of sheer shock and amazement.

My mom and stepdad had gifted me a friend of my very own. They did not know how much of a friend to me this puppy would truly be.

Her name was Annabelle. They gave her the name at the Humane Society, but there was something about her name that was special to me. I kept her name the same and did my best to give her a better life.

I didn't realize that I might have been overcompensating at a young age, but something about Annabelle made me feel whole. When the Humane Society gave me the backstory on my puppy, I almost cried.

98~LISAMARIE THOMAS

She had been on an illegal dog breeding farm. They had found dozens of dogs being malnourished, abused, and forcibly made to repopulate, but they had saved most of the dogs.

Many of the dogs were outside; however, Annabelle was older, so although she was still being abused, they kept her in the house.

I could tell that Annabelle was traumatized; she would always find a secluded spot to hide in. For the first few months, every time we walked into the house, we would have to go looking for Annabelle.

Every time we would find her, she would back up into a corner as far as she could. Sometimes, she would shake, even when she was in my arms. It always would take a few minutes for her to realize that she was safe.

It took a while, but she finally opened up to us. Now, when I got home, she would run right up to the door. Sometimes I could hear her waiting from the other side of the door before I could step onto the porch.

WHEN GOD LET ME SPEAK~99

Eventually, she opened up to everyone in the house, and our home had become her safety net.

I had never felt more fulfilled, and something about the experience with Annabelle made the things in my life seem not as bad. She showed me how to care for someone and gave me the motivation to push past my struggles for someone else.

That was one of the major elements that I needed to get through life. I think Annabelle needed me in the same way that I needed her. We both found safety and comfort in each other. I took her almost everywhere I went. She was bigger than she needed to be in order to fit in my purse, but I got her in places she didn't belong, like Walmart.

We stayed in the comfort of my mom's home for a year until I left school. She came with me when I roomed with some girls and when my ex and I moved in together.

It seemed like every time I would be sad, she would just be there.

Anytime I needed her and anytime that she needed me, I would be there.

100~LISAMARIE THOMAS

It's kinda hard to believe that I'm talking about my dog, but it's so true.

Our relationship was so unique that I believe that GOD gave Annabelle to me for a reason. She prepared me to receive another blessing, my daughter.

My journey with Annabelle ended shortly before I found out that I was pregnant with my daughter.

The day before my doctor's appointment, Annabelle died.

XIII

God-Given

Lianna Michelle.

Lianna means "Daughter of the Sun" and is the diminutive

form of Eliana, which means "Jehovah is God."

This chapter is for you, my love. It is both a testimony and a dedication to your life. Sometimes you just know when God has given something to you, or even someone.

At this moment in my life, I've only been your mother for six and a half years to date. However, you have saved my life more times than a few.

101

102~LISAMARIE THOMAS

This chapter might be a little long, but it's worth it. You are worth it. Your life is so special. You are so special that the Devil has tried to take you away from me. He didn't even want me to receive the blessing that you are. He wanted to see me die, but God gave me you and allowed me to live.

This reflection is not to make you sad. In fact, it is the opposite. At whatever age you read and can understand this, feel empowered. This reflection shows the strength that God put in your soul.

He gave you the ability to be more powerful than an entity made to destroy your life, and that's the most amazing thing I've ever heard. I told the story of your birth in Turned Out. I was eighteen, and it stacked the odds against me pretty high.

Things weren't the best between me and your biological dad, Mike, and truthfully, his purpose may not have been to be in your life, and that's perfectly fine. I don't fault him for it. We were both pretty young and did not know what we wanted in our lives.

WHEN GOD LET ME SPEAK~103

We thought we wanted to be together but hadn't discovered who we were yet. The stress during the pregnancy complicated things. I would listen to classical music and jazz. I would even put the headphones on my belly while I cooked, cleaned, or worked.

I wanted your journey here to be soothing. More comforting than what was waiting on the outside. There was argument after argument. My hormones were everywhere, and I could be irate sometimes, but I expected a love that I hadn't experienced yet, and that was a lot to ask for.

Arguments got worse, and at one point, I can admit, I had been the aggressor. After an argument one night, he called the police on me. Though, I just wanted us to be a family more than anything. At five months pregnant, I went to Dougherty County Jail for disorderly conduct.

We were both handling the pregnancy in different ways, and I was adamant that no one was going to be in his life but me.

104~LISAMARIE THOMAS

There were also feelings of inadequacy. I didn't feel attractive anymore, and I don't think he was ready for everything that came with a relationship and family then. This is not to place the blame of a rocky relationship with anyone.

This is to show you how many factors we were dealing with. The interesting part about my relationship with Mike is that it didn't mess up your life. It actually made things better. The tumultuous years of us figuring out what we wanted.

Through your life, I had discovered and experienced both developmental and natural love. This built my character as a parent. It took a lot of perception to realize that was a blessing. God blessed me with some great doctors and nurses, even though I could only afford care at my local health department.

They took great care of you and me. They noticed something was wrong with me right away. I wanted to be prepared for you, so I was working a lot.

WHEN GOD LET ME SPEAK~105

I had been working at the Chuck E. Cheese in the mall for a couple of years, but I was spending way too much time on my feet. The days went on, and I gained more and more water weight.

There were days that my feet were so swollen that I couldn't get out of the bed. I was still only five months pregnant.

Shortly after, we found they diagnosed me with preeclampsia and sent me to the hospital to wait out the rest of my pregnancy on bed rest.

I was midway through my college semester, and I was taking classes online. I really wanted to show you I could be a wonderful mom and take care of you. I wanted to prove to both you and myself that I could provide a better life for the both of us.

Every night, I was up. I was trying to write papers and finish assignments. Then, on October 21, 2012, the Devil tried to take you from me. His attempt was so large that it was enough to take both of us. Mike was there. He moved quickly and alerted the doctors when he knew something was wrong.

106~LISAMARIE THOMAS

I can give him credit for that. Even though I was tripping off the anesthetic, I could hear the urgency in the doctors' voices.

They were afraid that I might have a seizure. I needed to be sedated as quickly as possible. They were going to deliver you via an emergency C-section. Let's stop for a second. This might not be relevant, but here's an interesting fact. You were born in Albany, GA. Phoebe Putney Memorial Hospital is the name. Around the time you were born, they were the fifth worst hospital in the entire country.

Let's remember our talk about perception. Don't look at this the wrong way. Don't be sad or embarrassed. This is a part of your testimony.

The Devil tried to set you up to fail, but he has no power over God.

Regardless of where you were, God implemented the right people to be there.

They had the right resources, ability, courage, motivation, and intentions. It was according to God's plan, and they still saved our lives.

WHEN GOD LET ME SPEAK~107

You were born with a protection over your life. I knew that when the Devil tried again.

The next time was pretty quick and pretty obvious. To start, you only stayed in the NICU for eighteen days before you pulled the tube and started feeding yourself. It was amazing. You had no fear. Mike and I were so happy when we finally put you in the car and headed home.

We only lived about ten minutes from the hospital and were about three miles from being there. Mike had this old-school Jaguar he was crazy about. He carefully drove down the road, and we were coming to a stop when we noticed a car driving fast behind us. We both may have gone into shock for a second, not knowing what to expect.

The car kept coming, and Mike moved up further to the light, while trying not to run it. About two inches behind us, the car came to a screeching halt. It happened so fast.

We both looked at each other and looked back at you. You slept peacefully in the back seat, at only five pounds.

108~LISAMARIE THOMAS

Something in both of us knew we were protected, but it didn't make the feelings any less unsettling. We made it home safely, but three days later, we were on the way to the store. The same thing happened again, with an unfamiliar car. Three days after that, the same thing happened. It completely rocked Mike and me to our core.

We thought that somebody wanted us dead, maybe a person. I thought it might have been the girl that he was having an affair with, but none of it made sense. Who would want us to die? The person behind the wheel of the first car was a white man.

Ever since then, you were healthy. You have thrived and grown into a beautiful person. You are extremely intelligent. God gave you those qualities for you to be someone great. I noticed that when the Devil could not take you from me, he was going to take me from you.

One way or the other, he was persistent and determined.

WHEN GOD LET ME SPEAK~109

When I reflect on this story, I realize how blessed I am. It took a few more experiences for me to see that God had been walking with me. He is walking with you too. Your heart is pure, and it gives you the joy to see the beauty of the world. That is worth more than anything. I know God put you here to share that with all of His people.

As a mother, the more I paid attention to life, I learned the purpose of my child. Now, my life's goal is to push her to be who she is born to be. I knew my parents loved me, but they weren't able to do that. However, I'm in a better position and able to take care of my child, so that's what I want to do. She deserves that.

Many of us are lost. I don't think I'm a perfect parent. My daughter went through so much in her short period of life. Nothing directly bad happened to her, but I always felt that it wasn't fair that she had to see my tragedy.

It took me being lost and almost destroyed to even realize that I had a purpose.

110~LISAMARIE THOMAS

I want us to do something different as parents and as people. My daughter's life showed me that living for me is not selfish. I spent so much time looking for love and fulfillment. I thought that the life that I wanted to give my children had to be a mom and a dad. The same mother and father, with significant jobs and married.

What I had to remember was that what God has for you is for you. The best thing that I could do for my children was to be the best mom that I could be. I have to love myself and make myself happy. That is the best way to give the ultimate love to them.

As a parent, I could focus on what made my daughter happy and tune into those things.

It took almost five years, but I finally got there, and it feels so much better. I'm putting my energy into what God gave me. He didn't give me relationships; he didn't give me a man. He gave me myself and my children. He gave me my purpose and the plan for my life.

WHEN GOD LET ME SPEAK~111

He allowed me to discover my purpose through my children. I have God and maybe even the Devil to thank for that.

The tragedy molded me into a better and stronger person. I had to take that into consideration. When I finally focused on myself, I wrote.

I wrote an entire book and never knew that I would be an author.

It felt great, even if no one ever read a word.

Everything about that turning point in my life was God-given.

XIV

The Man in the Dark

It took me a while to gather up the strength to write this chapter. I would stare at the title sometimes, but I just wasn't ready to write it yet.

It's Sunday night, though, on March 31, 2019, 10:44 PM, and I think I'm ready. You guys know that I'm scary by now, right?

Okay, cool.

Well, here's another thing that I might be afraid of. I might be afraid to die. It's not just that I'm afraid to die; it's more so that I'm afraid of how I might die. I'm afraid to experience a pain so great that it brings death.

112

WHEN GOD LET ME SPEAK~113

I couldn't imagine what that would feel like, except for childbirth.

I honestly think that that may have been my reasoning for even contemplating the thought of suicide. I did not solely base it on the fact that I hated my circumstances, as much as I did. It was also because I felt that my circumstance could cause my death, and I wanted control instead.

Is that worth eternal damnation? That's an open-ended question because, obviously, there's only one way to find out the answer, and I'm still kicking.

Moving on.

There was a period that I stopped having dreams, and I never thought much about it until my dreams would period- ically return.

There was something weird about them, though. The first time I noticed that there was something different about my dreams was when I was pregnant with Leah, at 17.

114~LISAMARIE THOMAS

I was sleeping, and I finally had another dream. It was ter- rifying. Everything was dark, and I saw myself. I was at home, and I was pregnant and sitting on my bed.

I looked towards the door and saw a man standing there. He realistically wasn't very far away. It seemed to me, though, that he was far away because I couldn't make anything out about him. He was tall, but he was just black. I'm not talking about skin color clothes.

He was just black, black nothingness from what I could see.

There was immediate fear in my body. Everything about his energy was evil. I knew he had no good intentions for me. Then he got closer. I didn't run at first, but eventually, my brain told me to run. I got up and ran towards the kitchen, where there was a back door.

Then he came for me. I don't know if he was running, flying, or teleporting, but I did not know how I was going to get away from him. He got close to me when I got into the kitchen, and he had a knife, a big one.

WHEN GOD LET ME SPEAK~115

As I expected, he went straight for me, but he didn't stab me. I got out the door and ran down the street.

He was still chasing me; I tripped, and he caught my leg. I tried crawling away from him, and the knife came for me again, but he didn't get me. I ran down the street, and again, he was right behind me.

I don't know what made me turn around, but I did, and he was there. Nothing, nothing was there with a knife to my belly.

Then it was over.

I woke up screaming. I ran into my mom's room and woke her up. I was so scared that I couldn't even tell her what I had seen. I didn't know how to describe it on impact, as I'm able to years later. I didn't know what that meant.

Was somebody trying to kill me? Was somebody trying to kill my baby? The only thing I could do next to my mom was to hug her and cry. She was panicking because that's just her nature as a Cancer.

116~LISAMARIE THOMAS

I could finally tell her what I saw, and she calmed down. She could calm me down by telling me that what I was seeing wasn't real.

She told me that sometimes you have crazy dreams while

you're pregnant, and she told me I was safe. I still wanted to sleep in the bed with her, but I felt better.

Until the night it happened again, and I was home alone.

I felt paralyzed as I lay there face to face with the same person. He wanted to kill me again; this time, he had a gun. He pointed it right at me, dead in my face. I was pregnant still, in this dream. Then as I stood there unable to move, he slowly lowered the gun and pointed it at my belly.

There was nothing I could do except to back away as far as I could. Within two seconds, it balled me up in a corner, just hoping that I wouldn't die. There were about five seconds of fear before it was over. Just like that, I was back in my bed, just lying there. I couldn't believe that I was alive.

WHEN GOD LET ME SPEAK~117

I know that seems like a stretch, but these dreams were so real. They felt like reality, like I was standing there. I could feel the adrenaline, and I could feel the fear. They held me captive, and I could only leave when it was over.

I'm not sure what was more terrifying—the feeling of being trapped in your own mind or the possibility that what I was dreaming was real.

From that point on, I started living with the possibility that one day, someone might kill me. I didn't know how or why. I couldn't count the number of times now that I have had a gun pointed at me or directly in my face. There's something about death that's interesting.

In my lowest points, I've wanted to die. However, every time it has faced me with death, I wanted to live. There's one situation that makes me add one more line of perception into this analysis.

Apart from dreams or other people, there was one time I thought I might die of natural causes.

It's kind of a funny story, actually.

118~LISAMARIE THOMAS

One afternoon, I was laughing with my boyfriend and drinking a pink lemonade.

Out of nowhere, the lemonade goes down the wrong pipe. I literally have half a cup of lemonade stuck in my windpipe.

It brought me to my knees for almost a minute; I was choking. I couldn't breathe and couldn't say anything. It was then that I felt my oxygen levels depleting.

I could faintly hear my boyfriend telling me to hold my arms in the air. I could feel him trying to put my arms in the air.

At that moment, part of my mind wanted to save myself, and the other half wanted to let myself go.

It may not make sense, but a person's sense of control is more important than it's made out to be.

That's exactly what it was, control.

WHEN GOD LET ME SPEAK~119

In that moment, I was equally afraid of living, as I was of dying.

At that moment, I felt I had a choice, without the pain of murder or the consequences of killing myself.

I didn't have long to determine how important my daughter's life was to me or how important my son's life was.

I had very little time to figure out if it would still punish me for making a conscious decision to let myself go.

Was I trying to outsmart God?

I was way too impatient to wait on my fate. Hell, I had the opportunity right then, but no.

I had slipped away, but I have come back, and I wanted another try.

I would not quit yet.

How could I?

I wasn't about to run away from life this time.

120~LISAMARIE THOMAS

1. V

5 AM

This is a pretty short story, but it's one about protection.

One thing that God has kept showing me in every moment in my life or with every decision that I've made was that he was there for me.

He has been there for me more than any human or pet I've ever known, alive or dead.

Not only was he always there for me, but I also noticed that God did something that no one else could do. He protected me everywhere I was.

121

122~LISAMARIE THOMAS

It didn't matter if I called on Him or if I had moved ahead of Him. He had provided a covering for me.

I knew God wasn't always happy with my decisions or with my impatience, but He had still wanted me here. Whether I wanted to be here.

Most of all, I never had to explain to him why I did something. I knew God knew my heart and knew my intentions. I just didn't know what he had planned for me every time he saved me.

"God, why do You keep saving me?"

I moved to Atlanta for the first time as an adult in 2013. I was so excited because I felt like I was starting a brand new chapter in life. I had just had a daughter and turned eighteen. I was also leaving a relationship with my daughter's father, and I felt like my life was falling together again.

I was even getting an apartment, and I could say, at that moment, I was genuinely happy.

My daughter was staying with her father for a few months until I got my apartment, but every Friday, when I was off,

I would drive to Albany to visit her. I could stay for the weekend and head back to Atlanta on Sunday evening. Normally, I would leave around seven or eight, at the latest.

WHEN GOD LET ME SPEAK~123

I could get back into town around ten or eleven. That schedule afforded me enough time to get enough sleep and get ready for work on Monday morning.

One Sunday, I was running late getting back. We had done so much over the weekend, and I had missed spending time with my family and friends. Most of all, I had missed being able to see my daughter every day, and I was missing the days that I couldn't see her growing. I had planned to head out around nine, but things got later and later.

We had gone to Aunt Val's to have dinner with our other family members, so I figured I could leave around eleven at the latest.

I finally ended up leaving at 1:30 in the morning. Everyone wished me safe travels, and I stopped by the Pilot Gas Station right off of Highway 300. From there, I would have to drive thirty miles down a long dark road to reach the main Interstate 75. Then, I would be three hours away from home.

That drive is always the most boring part of the trip. It's also not a very safe trip to make at night. There's very minimal traffic.

124~LISAMARIE THOMAS

The speed limit shifts between thirty-five and fifty-five the complete way there, and there are plenty of deer. That night, though, I was in a rush. I didn't have time to think about all the cautionary things; I barely thought about getting stopped. I knew I needed to keep this job to get an apartment and keep my car note. I did sixty almost the whole way there.

I was driving by this gas station that looked to be closed. I had wanted to stop in and grab something to drink, but that would not happen. I needed to keep myself awake. I listened to some music on my phone. I had a little android and had the TIDAL app, so that would work perfectly, but I had no clue where my aux cord was.

I'm trying to look for my cord and stay focused, and before you even go there, I know that's dumb. Okay, so I end up finding it on the floor. Now, I'm looking at the road and just trying to stick my cord in my phone. The first time, I looked up at the road, and I saw nothing there. Then, I glanced down briefly to make sure the cord was in. The second time that I looked up, I was about ten feet from something white, just sitting in the road.

I almost didn't stop. I mean, I did, but I think my brain was trying to process what was in front of me.

WHEN GOD LET ME SPEAK~125

Something in my brain decided that there was no time for that, and my foot pressed on the brake. I'm only five feet away now. The headlights on my car are shining brightly, allowing me to see what's blocking the road. I couldn't be more surprised at what was there.

It was the trailer of a semi-truck.

It had attempted to make a U-Turn. I'm not sure what happened with the truck, but it didn't seem like anyone was in it. There were no lights on or anything. The truck was just there. I know I'm not crazy. That truck had not been there before. I didn't even know what had just happened. I just sat there in a daze, wondering what was inside the truck? What would have happened if I would have hit it? Where did it come from?

Once I collected my thoughts, I had to drive through the other lane in order to get around and reach the highway. Interstate 75 was another eight miles away, and I had to sit down for a second. I had to allow myself to process what had just happened.

I drove for another three miles before I saw an open gas station. I couldn't even stop; I was too happy to be alive.

126~LISAMARIE THOMAS

XVI

The Dream of Everlasting Life

Dream Big and I will Go Beyond That.

Dreams are interesting.

They are spiritual and involuntary, yet intentional discernment from another energy paradigm.

Many times, they are hard to describe or even remember, but there was one dream that may have possibly told me about my future.

I was nine years old.

127

128~LISAMARIE THOMAS

I was living with my Mommy Lorraine, and would talk to my dad on the phone from time to time.

There was this one particular occasion that I called him early in the morning.

It was around seven in the morning.

This is how our conversation went:

"Hey, Daddy, Daddy, good morning."

He told me, in the sleepiest voice, "Good morning, baby."

I had just woken up. I was the most excited to talk to him; I had something that I needed to tell him.

He asked if I could call him back when he woke up in a couple of hours, but I couldn't wait. I had to let him know, right then, what I had seen.

He obliged, of course, and listened to me. He asked me about what I saw, and I told him about the dream I had the night before.

This is how it went:

"Me and my friend were walking down the street. We were just walking and walking.

The streets were real quiet, Daddy. You know, those things on the trees. Like cobwebs, just rolling down the street. But Daddy, listen to this. Nobody was on the street at all. We kept walking, and we were passing these different cities, and nobody was there. The entire country looked old. I looked in the buildings, and everything was dark and sad.

Me and my friend were confused, and we just kept walking. I was wondering where everyone was. I didn't even know where we were going, Daddy, but I felt like I knew what direction to keep walking. We finally stopped walking, and I looked up. We had walked all the way to Washington, D.C.

We got to a church, and the church was so big. It was like the only thing there. We were kind of nervous, but we walked in. Daddy, you wouldn't believe it. Everybody in the entire country was inside the church.

It was really everybody. There were gangsters and thugs right at the front door. They were throwing all of their money, drugs, and guns on the ground. They were crying. They kept saying that they don't want to do that anymore.

We walked towards the front of the church. It was so crowded. These important people were in the front rows, and everybody was listening to somebody talking. I could hear them, but I couldn't see them, so we went closer.

When we got to the front, we saw President Bush and his

wife. I finally saw who was talking, and guess who it was, Daddy?

It was you, and God was standing behind you."

After I had finished, I had to call my dad's name to make sure he was still there. A few seconds later, he told me he was. I didn't know what my dream meant or why I had it, but I felt I needed to share that with him. He didn't sound tired anymore. In fact, he sounded wide awake. He asked me to repeat my dream for him, and I told him everything once again.

That dream took a backseat in my mind for years. It wasn't until I was around twenty-one that I thought about it again. There was one question that I always had but could never come closer to the answer.

How did I know that was God?

What did He look like?

Was He a person or a spirit?

WHEN GOD LET ME SPEAK~131

I've tried, desperately, many times to remember that dream. I wanted to visualize it again. I wanted to see it again from a mature perspective. It never happened, though.

Something about that dream has always been profound to me. Something about it told me that God had a plan, and we may have been a part of that.

I never thought that the dream was literal, but there was a message.

But what exactly was God trying to say to me? Around the same time, a few months later, I was attending a Sunday morning church service. There was a guest speaker there, and towards the end of service, she said that she had a special word for me.

The speaker told me I had a gift of discernment. She said that my gift was powerful and that God had a plan for me, but the Devil would be after me.

At that moment in my life, I didn't put too much thought into it, but nowadays, I think about the words she spoke to me.

132~LISAMARIE THOMAS

XVII

Trending Topic

There are two primary types of people that do drugs. One-half are people that want to experiment, and the other half are people looking for any way to cope with anything that they might go through.

I honestly don't know which person I was when I first tried any drugs. I think I might have been in between, trying to find myself and just wanting to be happy by any means. The first drug that I ever tried was Molly.

133

134~LISAMARIE THOMAS

I heard about it in 2013, right around the time that I moved to Atlanta for the first time. It was in 2015, though, that I had indulged. I'm pretty sure you remember Peanut from Turned Out, right?

Well, it was right after me and my daughter's dad had broken up for the last time. I had spent the last five years of my life being in a relationship and being a mother that I hadn't even found out who I was as a person yet. What I found was the person who I never wanted to become. I plan to be very explicit in this chapter.

Slight Disclaimer:

If you're too young or too religious, or have any objections, I encourage you to move on to the next chapter.

It's about to get real.

The first time I tried Molly was a crazy and very short-lived experience. My daughter was at my dad's for the weekend, and I went to hang out with my home girl.

She's always with some guy that's taking care of her, so when she introduced me to her guy friend, it wasn't a surprise, and he seemed cool.

WHEN GOD LET ME SPEAK~135

He had a really nice SUV and took us out to get food. He had plenty of weed for us to smoke just sitting in the car, so we were chilling.

We hung out at this wing spot, right by the Walmart on Old Nat.

He lived in Union City, which wasn't too far from where we were. Peanut told me how he had this nice condo with a jacuzzi tub, and we were welcome to come over for a while.

I was a little skeptical, but I was newly single, kid-free, and young, so what the hell? Right?

Probably not. Things got a little interesting right before we left for Union City. Peanut looked at me with this mischievous smile and said, "Hold out your hand." I look up, and I'm like, "What the hell for?"

She goes, "You always ask too many questions, just gimme your hand."

I gave it to her.

She put something in my hand that was crystal-looking. I was like, "What the fuck is this?" I almost threw it when I said,

"I'm not doing crack or no shit like that." Then she gave me her I'm-not-stupid face and said, "It's not crack, smart-ass, it's just Molly. Chill out. Do you want it or not?"

136~LISAMARIE THOMAS

I thought about it, for what seemed like forever, to everyone else. Then I finally tried it.

Don't say it. I know it was stupid, okay?

What I felt like on it, though…

That was the most surprising thing ever.

There was so much euphoria. My body felt so light, and I felt so open, like I could tell anyone anything, and I did. I really told my life to everyone listening, secrets that I had told no one else. I had put it all out there without even thinking about it.

One thing that was clear was I had little to no fear. I felt like I could do anything. I think I've been craving that feeling my entire life, and it was easy to get addicted to.

Everything felt good to me. I did not know what it was doing to my brain.

It wasn't until about a week later that I realized how angry I was becoming and how dependent I had become.

I had spent almost every day hanging out with a guy that was just buying me food and giving me drugs.

WHEN GOD LET ME SPEAK~137

I had become completely out of my mind.

On a normal day, I would think about my daughter a lot;

even if I was at work and knew she was safe, I would still think about her.

In the past week, she hadn't really crossed my mind. I realized that, but the drugs were too powerful, and I wanted them.

In the next coming days, I almost felt like I needed them. It became a real problem, really fast. I had gone to see my daughter; she had been at the babysitter for almost a week.

I could barely keep paying for it, but I paid for another week. I told her it was because I had been working overtime lately, but in reality, my life had become work and drugs.

I was spiraling downward. I was becoming the person who I said I never wanted to be. I was becoming the parent that I had promised myself that I would never be. I wasn't being fair to my daughter, but my judgment was seriously clouded.

It wasn't until a full two weeks later that I saw what was happening to me. I had lost a ton of weight and had missed three days of work.

138~LISAMARIE THOMAS

You would think that was enough, but there was something else that happened that flipped the switch for me.

My dad and I are very close, as I'm sure you know by now. I have always had a major respect for him, and we've always had very good communication.

I've never had to raise my voice at him, but the drugs and anger were consuming me. One day, we had a discussion about fixing the packaging for our product, Extend-A-Brush.

We were working on a distribution deal with Sherwin-Williams, and I had designed the packaging, so there were a few things that I needed to fix. Usually, I was very open to my dad's suggestions and criticism because it was always constructive.

I felt defensive, though, and I couldn't be receptive to anything that he was saying. I wouldn't listen to anything that he was saying; I just yelled, and honestly, I didn't even know what I was yelling about.

WHEN GOD LET ME SPEAK~139

What I knew was that I wasn't myself, and that scared me more than anything. It was at that moment that I decided that my life was more. It was then that I had determined that my life had more value. It was then that I decided I would never do Molly ever again, but I slipped.

I met the father of my son, working at Ford, and he was selling weed. It wasn't until we had become intimate that he told me he also sold Molly. I swore to myself that I would never touch it, but I felt like, maybe this time, I could control it. I will not lie; I controlled it much better than the first time. However, I still bit off much more than I could chew.

I finally realized that when I became pregnant with my son. I couldn't do any drugs anyway, but I didn't plan to have any more children.

I felt that under the influence, I was reckless, impulsive, and unconventional. Those thoughts made me lose the desire to bring circumstances into my life.

After that, I never touched Molly again.

140~LISAMARIE THOMAS

I thought that my life had ended when I learned I was pregnant for a second time, but little did I know that my life was just beginning.

It wasn't until I fell into Boss' trap that I used drugs again. This time, it was ecstasy pills.

When I listened to him, Boss would buy me weed. That was God-given because marijuana had to have stopped me from killing myself more times than I've actually tried.

This one day, though, the guy that sold Boss weed told him he also had x pills. We call them beans. I asked Boss if I could have one. He actually slapped the shit out of me.

He asked me if I wanted to be more horny when I hit the plays. He asked me if I was trying to be on some freaky shit. I gave him my honest answer. I told him I had taken one before, and it made me feel calm, sometimes creative.

I told him I could help him with his projects, like his CD cover.

WHEN GOD LET ME SPEAK~141

Let's pause for a second.

I know you're wondering why I offered to do this.

1. I needed to persuade him to buy me something more to cope with what was happening.
2. I needed something to take my mind off of what was happening, and that would take no effort and about fifteen minutes of my time.

Back to the story.

I told him I had a slightly traumatic past,

and I told him about the research that I did.

142~LISAMARIE THOMAS

Ecstasy pills were first sold to soldiers in the seventies to treat the symptoms of PTSD.

PTSD is post-traumatic stress disorder. That is anybody that has suffered and/or living with a traumatic background or experience and can negatively affect their physical, social, or psychological disposition.

Continuing my explanation to Boss, I told him that not everyone's the same. I told him that everyone doesn't do drugs for the same reason.

He seemed to understand my explanation in some unusual manner. In about a week's time, he brought me 3.5 grams of weed and three ecstasy pills.

I took one and felt better. When I hit the plays, it didn't feel different. The only difference was, I could leave in my mind. I got to a point that I was literally not there anymore.

There was some sense of euphoria when I was alone.

That helped me parent Leah better through all the chaos. WHEN GOD LET ME SPEAK~143

I will not lie; my biggest fear was becoming an addict. I didn't want to let my daughter down. I didn't want to let my children down. I tried to control it, and I did for a while. I never got out of control, but I was taking as many as I needed to cope with my everyday life.

I feared so many things. I was afraid to keep living in my circumstance. I was afraid of spiraling out of control. I was afraid that I would be a poor parent. They would catch me doing drugs and that I would lose my children.

I was still being the best mom that I could be and protecting my daughter the best way I knew how.

I didn't feel that I deserved to lose my children, and it petrified me.

I kept doing drugs, using the best moderation that I could.

By the time the situation with Boss ended, my drug use had gone down.

I was never an addict, but I would increase my usage based on my stress level.

144~LISAMARIE THOMAS

I'll honestly admit that I didn't stop completely, although I slowed almost all the way down.

There was something that I felt when I took the pills that would allow me to keep going.

I could be in a different head space when I needed to be, so that every traumatic thought, fear, flash back, and experience didn't plague me.

I feel a little guilty about that, but it never affected my parenting.

How I thought about it, I would be in a worse situation having to pay for counseling and tripping off psych meds. It was the most affordable way out of the living hell in my mind.

I guess I will take that chance. I just wanted the opportunity to be a better person.

I needed to become sane again. I felt I needed some kind of block in order to parent my children.

There was an enormous amount of risk, sure.

I felt that my inner person was worth that, though.

WHEN GOD LET ME SPEAK~145

I felt like she was suffering, like she was drowning, and I needed to save her.

I hoped and prayed that I could cope long enough to discover myself and grow into my authentic person.

I didn't want to steer myself in the wrong direction.

I prayed God would still love and protect me, even in this route I chose.

XVIII

Black Magic

This is a pretty long chapter, and it gets pretty deep.

I have warned you.

I say that because when I think about the events that occurred in this part of my life, I still get the chills. This is the part of life where I made one of the biggest mistakes I could ever make. Aside from any religious beliefs, I had walked away from God and danced with the Devil.

It all started when I met this guy named Chris.

146

WHEN GOD LET ME SPEAK~147

I was searching for a job, and I had experience in car sales, so I stopped in this place called Pars Cars to fill out an application.

I had on this brown pinstripe business suit, and I fixed my hair in a perfect bun. I was almost in my car when I saw him standing there.

He had on a business shirt and tie, but his frame was clear. I could see the definition of his arms through his long sleeves, he was dark-skinned, and that was my favorite, then he hit me with a perfectly white smile. Shit!

He nodded at me like he wanted me to hold on for a second, and you already know I stopped. I'm in overdrive right now, as he towers over me at a little over six feet. He asked me my name and what I was doing there. We had a little small talk, and he asked me to dinner. He asked me, "Do you smoke?"

I gave him a slight smile and told him I did, but I didn't drink. He liked that, and we met up later. He was only a few years older than me, but he seemed to have himself together, and I loved a man that had something going for himself. He had his own car, home, a decent paying job, he rapped as a hobby, and he seemed to have a very mysterious side.

I think that might be what attracted me to him the most.

I never knew what it was, but it was something that made me want to know what was going on in his head. He was so hard to read; I had chalked it up to him being a Scorpio. It was in their nature to be a little mysterious, but this was something much more. Something in me had to know, and to this day, I wish I hadn't.

When we met up, I was even more interested in him. He seemed like a good mix of the guys I had attractions to. He didn't seem gangster or "thugged out," but he had a respectable presence, and he was street smart.

I had a thing for the thugs too, but I was trying to be on the straight and narrow as much as possible.

The thing was, Chris didn't need that. He was confident, borderline cocky, but it didn't show with me.

He was a loner, but he was great in the professional or social setting.

He had a deep voice that captivated me every time he spoke.

He wasn't needy, and he had just enough affection that it wasn't overbearing, but it kept me wanting more.

He was just everything it seemed like, but you never know what people are really hiding or who they truly are.

That's the scary part of life and sometimes the most un-considered part of life.

We hung out for a few months, and everything was going great between us. I had just gotten a new position at the Terry-Cullen Chevrolet off of Battle Creek Road in Jones-boro. He didn't stay far from there, right down 138.

When my daughter Leah went to the sitter on the week-ends, I would stay over at his place. It eventually became a regular thing for us. There was this one night in particular, though, that he left and went to a friend's place. I had to work an extra shift in the morning and caught up on some sleep at his house until he got back.

He left around ten and came back at about one in the morning. I was sleeping pretty light because I wasn't home and woke up as soon as he walked into the room. He took some weed out, rolled a blunt, and told me about his night. He had fun. He asked me if I was okay at the house, and I said, "Yeah, I got a pretty good nap in."

150~LISAMARIE THOMAS

He was like, "Cool. I just wanted to make sure. There's normally someone here, but she probably wasn't because I was gone." Immediately, my mind was in-between scared and angry because I knew he didn't have any roommates. So, who the hell was he talking about?

Then, I felt a little stupid because he had two sisters and a mom. They probably check on his place when he's not there. I just asked.

I was not expecting his answer, though...

He tells me, "I have a friend that follows me around. She's been here for a long time. I don't know why she does or why she's here. She won't bother you, though, unless you do something bad to me or something, but it's nothing to worry about."

Let me say this before we go any further.

I've known this man for months now and been in this house too many times to count. It's the wee hours of the morning, and this is a grown-ass man telling me this.

This can only be one of three things.

- He's joking and trying to scare me.

- He's completely fucking delusional.

- He's serious, and I'm about to get really creeped out.

I wish I was a fly on the wall to see my face because I know I was looking really stupid. I don't even remember what my response was, but I know it was utter confusion.

"What do you mean?" was all I could ask.

I didn't go back there for a while. A couple of weeks later, I finally stayed the night again. I figured I was being stupid and just needed to get over it. That night, he said nothing about the situation, but I never felt the same in his house again.

I frequented his house more often, and the less afraid I became. I didn't know if there was anyone or any entity around me I couldn't see, but I felt safe, and that was all that mattered at the moment. Chris and I grew closer and closer. He was very closed off about himself and his private life at first, but he had finally opened up to me.

Initially, I only learned tidbits about him. The things that you could expect to learn about a person.

152~LISAMARIE THOMAS

I learned about his favorite things and his family. You know. Basic.

One day, though, he finally showed me who he was. His house was being renovated, and he came to stay at my apartment for about a week. I noticed that he did a lot of reading on his phone, so I was interested in what he liked to look at.

When I asked, he nonchalantly told me he was reading about magic. He had to see the spark of curiosity in my eyes and the questions forming because he sat up slightly and gave me his attention. Then I asked questions like, "Why are you reading about that? Do you do magic? Isn't that like witchcraft or something? How does that even work?"

He seemed to like the fact that I was interested and gave me the answers to my questions with no hesitation. He seemed comfortable and confident, as always, in his decision and explanation. That was honest, provoking without him knowing.

He explained to me he did magic, but it wasn't Evil magic. It was "Black Magic."

He told me he had tried some money spells using black magic that had come back on him in the most negative way.

WHEN GOD LET ME SPEAK~153

He told me that after he learned about the unique magic that he could do, he went with "White Magic."

He didn't say white magic was blessed, but he made it apparent that black magic was cursed.

It honestly seemed simpler than I had imagined.

Then he explained astral projection and how we could separate ourselves from our bodies during sleep. He explained as if our conscious soul could watch our bodies in action-like analysis, and that was compelling to me.

It wasn't long before I had dabbled in magic myself. I never did much. I read a couple of spells in my head, and I did a lot of research to start off. The more I read about astral projection, the more interested I became in wanting to try it.

The idea was fascinating to me that I could tap into and view the world and myself from a different platform, from my soul. I found it amazing to think that my consciousness could willingly travel through different planes.

154~LISAMARIE THOMAS

I thought about all the possibilities. I wondered if I could gain more control over my life. I wondered whether this ability could give me the advantage that I needed to have a better life.

It was right after Leah was born that I noticed I didn't dream anymore.

When I did, it was every blue moon, and the dreams were in vivid color, almost lifelike. I think that was a major factor in the concept of astral projection. I wanted to know what else was going on in my mind that I didn't know about.

I wanted to know what else I could do. For the first time, I felt that I truly had some power, and that feeling was empowering and refreshing, but it also could lead to my destruction.

So, I gave that a try first. Nothing happened the first time. In fact, nothing ever happened, and I was pretty bummed out.

Then, I said a spell out loud for the first time.

I tried a spell for blessings first. I just wanted to see what would happen, but yet again, nothing.

I sort of gave up at that point and went back to schedule programming.

WHEN GOD LET ME SPEAK~155

One night, I came home from work to my one-bedroom apartment.

Leah's crib was in my living area. I had set it up as a playroom/bedroom for her. She was about ten months old. After cooking, I laid Leah down to sleep for the night.

Then, I took a shower, lay across the bed, rolled a blunt, and checked my Facebook.

As I'm scrolling down Facebook, I hear the weirdest noise. It sounds like Leah is crying. Normally, her cry wouldn't sound weird to me, but there was something about this cry that was different and unsettling.

I'm walking to the living room and, I feel my anxiety rising, and the pit of my stomach is hollow. And that's when I saw her.

My daughter was lying there in her crib, screaming. Her eyes were closed shut like she was sleeping, and her face was as red as an apple. Her cry had turned into a scream; it was like a blood-curdling scream.

That's when I went to pick her up, and I thought I was going to die because I couldn't feel her.

She's in my arms, but I feel no life in her body.

156~LISAMARIE THOMAS

Yet her soul was conscious and trapped. I didn't look at it that way, as it was happening because it scared me shitless. I did not know what was happening to my daughter and why. However, I knew she was still there, even though she wasn't.

I ran into my room and sat on the bed with her rocking back and forth, screaming for her to wake up. I asked her if she could hear my voice. No response, and she continued to scream. I shook her gently enough that it could wake her up from her sleep. Her small body was limp, as she went back and forth, then she fell lifelessly back into my arms. I thought she had died.

As I cried, she cried again. Then her cries got louder and louder. They eventually resorted back to screams, and I couldn't take it anymore. I had to find some help for my child. I held her close to me as I stood up and gathered my purse and phone. I put them across my shoulder and made my way to the living room to get my car keys.

Within a second, things changed.

WHEN GOD LET ME SPEAK~157

My dad had given me this rectangular coffee table for my apartment. He had owned it for years, and there was one leg that was a little wobbly, and I was used to the table almost falling, but tonight there was a presence there that would make itself known. I realized it right after I grabbed my keys.

My keys were on the couch, but I had half of a blunt sitting on that wobbly table, and Lord knows I would need it when I got situated. So, I went to grab it. The moment my hand reached toward the table, the entire table came crashing down. All the legs seemed to collapse, and everything on it was all over the floor.

I let out an involuntary scream and covered my daughter with a blanket. I ran out the door as fast as I could and down the hill to my car. I was being very careful while holding Leah. Then I felt something.

In the most literal sense, something grabbed my ankle hard. I was falling straight to the ground with my ten-month-old, head-first, and could only think of what I could do to save her.

158~LISAMARIE THOMAS

I put my hand over the back of her head; I had to have closed my eyes because when I opened them, we were between a rock and a hard place, literally, but something had saved us. There was a rock with a sharp tip that was half an inch away from the back of her head.

She would have died instantly. Somehow though, we stopped right before she hit the rock, and we were almost in mid-air. There were so many emotions going on in my head when I realized the extent of the situation and that we were alive, but something was nagging away at me. "Why didn't we hit the ground?

How did I instinctively cover the right spot on Leah's head? What was holding us in the air?"

I had a million thoughts as I hopped in my car, fastened myself and Leah in tight, and sped down Riverdale Road, heading to my dad's house.

I had to find some kind of peace and understanding. The first thing on my list though was being somewhere where God was present.

WHEN GOD LET ME SPEAK~159

From that day, I told myself that I could never

lose faith in him like that again. Magic was now a closed chapter in my life. I was going to be totally comfortable trusting the only entity with the best intention for my life, God.

A couple of years later, I introduced magic again through my spirituality. I felt an inner calling to find guidance. There was something inside of me that called on me to manifest the things that I am capable of.

It assured me they would inform me during my journey. I took on my spirituality in a way that focused on prayers, growing plants, and working with herbs.

I've learned some teachings of our ancestors that pushed them through slavery and oppression for hundreds of years.

I know you think I'm insane.

I would, if I were you.

160~LISAMARIE THOMAS

This time, though, things would be different.

This time, my understanding was different.

I guess we'll see what happens.

X I X

2020

The experiences in my life made me a much more humble person.

The older I became, the more I learned the value of acceptance and growth.

The lessons were not only learned from experiences. I also learned through self-analysis.

I carried so much pain with me that I reflected that pain every day.

I was bitter and cold. I had developed extreme anxiety and felt like everyone was against me.

161

162~LISAMARIE THOMAS

People surrounded me, but I constantly felt alone.

My self-worth had become lost, and it didn't seem like there was anything to gain.

Have you ever felt lost?

It's January 1st, 2020, at 5:40 PM, and I am here again. This time, reflecting on another year that changed me.

It seemed like, when I took my life back, I began facing the hardest tribulations.

It seemed like, when I tried to be a better person and a better parent, I had more issues with my children.

It seemed like, when I tried to become wiser, I became less intelligent.

To me, I was becoming a lost cause.

However, in reality, I was being rebuilt.

The year started with me moving back to Atlanta from Albany. I had gotten kicked out of school and was actively looking for somewhere to live.

WHEN GOD LET ME SPEAK~163

I had a car, a 2011 Malibu, and plans to better my life. My best friend at the time was moving with me, and I was actually happy.

It took a few months for us to find a place. My dad had a six-bedroom house. I had just gotten a position at Coach downtown. I had previously worked from home but took a leave of absence to move. Darren was still working from home; the plan was that Darren, Leah, and I were going to stay at my dad's house until they approved our apartment.

Darren was going to watch Leah while I worked until we moved.

This is where things turned sour. Darren decided he didn't want to stay there and wanted to live with his ex-boyfriend and his husband. His ex-boyfriend, Malcolm, was my childhood friend. This is actually how Darren and I met. After Darren and Malcolm were together for five years, they broke up, and Malcolm got married.

Well, although we were all friends. Malcolm and his new husband decided Darren was welcome to stay, but not me or Leah. This left us in a pretty fucked-up predicament.

Please excuse my language, but my best friend left us out to dry.

164~LISAMARIE THOMAS

He knew I needed to work in order to pay my half of the move-in costs. He knew that my last school check wouldn't cover it.

There was no one at my dad's house to watch Leah. This meant that I would lose my job before I even started it.

I had to find somewhere that I could go, that I could have a babysitter and a place to stay. I will not lie. At one point, I said fuck it, and just live with my dad. I could wait as long as I needed to get a place, and I was comfortable there, but I couldn't leave my best friend out to dry like that.

He was from St. Louis and wouldn't have anywhere to go if we didn't get a place.

I called my friends Flo and Trina; they were a couple and had a little girl.

We had all been friends and had basically all slept together before. I needed to see if someone could watch Leah while I worked.

They agreed to watch Leah and told me I could stay there too. It was Flo's house. His mom had given it to him. It was the house that he grew up in, that his mother and grandmother raised him in.

Everything worked out pretty well at first.

WHEN GOD LET ME SPEAK~165

Leah was home-schooled, and they both helped me with getting her work done. Flo woke up at five every morning to drive me an hour to work and back.

Then, he would pick me up in downtown Atlanta traffic at 3 PM.

Trina was a dancer, and Flo was a contractor, so they both made substantial money. Once my checks came in, I was making decent money, as well. Trina and I both had guys that worshiped the ground we walked and could get money every day. It was easy.

They had an open relationship.

To some, the relationship that we had all developed would seem complicated, but it worked. Our kids were happy. I was saving the money I made to move, working and paying the note and insurance on my car.

Within a week, things changed again. They denied the apartment that Darren and I had applied for.

We had to go back to the drawing board to find somewhere to live. I had already been at Flo and Trina's for a month, and this setback would extend it another month, at least.

166~LISAMARIE THOMAS

The money had become irrelevant, and there was more work to do.

To make matters worse, one day, Flo's mom popped up at the house. They had been putting the deed to the house in his name. She pulled the strings on that.

To be clear, she was taking the house back. I didn't know her, but she did not want me there. Thankfully, she said that it was okay if Leah stayed. Turns out, she had plans to move with her boyfriend when she gave him the house. The relationship failed, and she came back.

I had to figure out again how I was going to get to work. For a few days, I would have Flo just drive me to Camp Creek, about thirty minutes away, and slept at my dad's house. He would have to come get me in the morning and pick me up from work.

Since his mom didn't get home until between five-thirty and seven, I would ride back to the house with him to check on Leah.

To save gas and time, some days, I started sleeping in my car outside of their house. I didn't want to be far away from my daughter. Not to mention, I had been late for work four times that week, and I was three days out of training.

WHEN GOD LET ME SPEAK~167

My job was working with me, but things were getting hard. Darren and I had applied for another place and were waiting on the results. A week later, Flo's mom made up with her boyfriend, and she would stay there for days at a time. This made things a little easier.

That's when things took another dramatic turn. Flo found out that Trina has been cheating on him with his cousin. He was hurting, and she had become an alcoholic bitch. Every night, she stayed on the drunk shit and the night ended in an argument. When you mix in drugs, shit got pretty bad.

She started doing everything that she could to make me feel uncomfortable, and I was over it. I had no desire to be friends with her. You're probably about to call me a dirty bitch, but I digress, honestly.

Flo and I had become much closer friends and talked about everything. The way I set my character up, I'm not about to condone anything that's fucked up, period.

Although Flo and I were already sleeping together, we started to more and more. Both of our feelings got involved, but neither one of us was a bad person.

168~LISAMARIE THOMAS

I didn't want to feel like a home-wrecker. It wasn't like she wasn't aware that we were sleeping together, but she didn't have any clue how we felt about each other.

Sometimes things got so bad that we just stayed together all night in the car. Talking, laughing, and fixing everything that was wrong in each other's lives. We both knew that we had fallen in love.

We were both against him leaving Trina, though. For Serenity's sake.

Serenity was Trina's daughter; her father died, and Flo had been a father to her for five years. She was ten years old. However, Trina had also left Flo.

She had cheated on him with a friend of his previously. She had his friend put out a TPO or Temporary Protection Order against him and had also had him arrested for Aggravated Assault.

She had tried to hit him with a liquor bottle while drunk, fell, chipped her front tooth, and lied to say Flo beat her with a pistol. She had even been taking money from him and sneaking men in and out of his house.

WHEN GOD LET ME SPEAK~169

She was toxic.

As our relationship developed and theirs diminished, more events would occur.

I moved into my place about a month later. I ended up staying with them for about three months.

Once I moved into my place, that's where Flo and I would go to get away once the kids were sleeping. It was a thirty-minute drive from his house, but it was worth it every time. To get peace and sleep next to each other.

We were so in love; we tried to have a child. It complicated things with us, but we needed each other.

That's when another problem arose with my son.

I had been sticking to my custody agreement, regardless of my circumstance, and all I asked from his dad and grandmother was to let me speak to him for a few minutes.

When I called, they would send me to voicemail or hang up in my face.

170~LISAMARIE THOMAS

One day, I just couldn't take it anymore. I called that old bitch and gave her a piece of my mind. I told her that Elijah was my son, and I was going to follow her to the end of the earth until I got him back. I directly let her know that if she kept trying to restrain the relationship between my son and I, I would have no problem taking her life. I told her it would be worth it.

You don't even have to tell me I fucked up. About two months later, after having a Friendsgiving party at my apartment, I left with Flo and Trina. We were going to visit one of their friends. That's when I was stopped by the police for a busted headlight. They arrested me that night on a Terroristic Threats charge—a felony.

It was about one in the morning on Saturday. I went to Fulton County for about twelve hours. Then, I went to Henry County and was being held without bond. Thankfully, I saw the judge Monday morning. He dropped the felony to a misdemeanor charge of harassing phone calls.

He granted a signature bond and released me at about 3 PM on Monday morning. I called Flo, and he was there in about twenty minutes to pick me up.

Being in jail had to be one of the worst experiences of my life.

WHEN GOD LET ME SPEAK~171

However, I learned a precious lesson.

When I got home, I had issues with my best friend. His ex and his new husband had broken up. Darren moved his ex into our two bedroom apartment without even asking me.

Here's the thing; I didn't have a problem with it. Then, when I would bring Flo, Trina, or Serenity over with Leah, he would have an attitude.

He would have friends that stayed over for days. Sometimes, I would stay at Flo and Trina's, and he would text me to see if I could stay over at their house for the night. Our neighbors would tell me how there would be a bunch of guys all night, doing God knows what!

One night, for Serenity's birthday, we had a slumber party for the kids and brought three other little girls over. Darren acted like I had to consult him.

Even though both of our names were on the lease. I was over how he had been treating me. Flo and I had finally gotten pregnant. I was so stressed out that I lost the baby five weeks later.

172~LISAMARIE THOMAS

That's when he called me one day to let me

know his mom sold the house. He had to find an apartment to move in under two weeks. He asked if he could stay with me for a couple of weeks until his place was ready.

Naturally, I said yes.

It was Flo, Trina, and Serenity, and it was pretty cramped for a couple of weeks. Then, one night, Flo and Trina got into it. She left to sleep with the drug dealer. She came back the next morning at about 10 AM. Still drunk and yelling. She probably tried to fight everyone that night, and she would not be welcome back in my house.

However, I told her if she would calm down, she could come back in. She kept up with the bullshit. Flo ended up giving her some money, and she left again. She returned to get Serenity a few hours later and ended up moving back to New Jersey.

Another three weeks later, I got a work-at-home job for Williams-Sonoma. I went to pay the rent on a Friday morning with Darren, and when I came back, DFCS was at my house. Trina called Child Services and told them two pages of lies about Leah and my parenting.

WHEN GOD LET ME SPEAK~173

I wasn't able to go to work. The DFCS lady stayed for about two hours, talking with Leah, Flo, Darren, Malcolm, his ex, and me. She checked to make sure we had food, checked Leah's room, checked to make sure she was in an accredited home-schooling program. The visit went extremely well, thank God.

The DFCS worker left with no other questions.

Mission Failed, Bitch.

I was to take a training test for my job and missed it.

Williams-Sonoma took back their job offer, and it devastated me.

It took weeks, and they denied me for three positions. I had to go back to calling guys I knew and figuring out how to make money. I had to leave the house or have a date over around three in the morning after everyone was sleeping.

After being brutally raped in the house while everyone was sleeping, Darren treated me differently and acted like he was controlling everything in the house. We covered this event in the chapter Trickmaster.

174~LISAMARIE THOMAS

That irritated me to the highest level, and we were arguing all the time. It was the second of the month.

Flo and I had this heated argument, and Darren came out. He was working from home, so he asked us to calm down. We actually did. Malcolm then came out behind him and started yelling on the rah-rah shit.

Malcolm, Darren, and I ended up getting into it. Flo

bucked on Malcolm because he was acting like he was going to put his hands on me. The next day, Darren and Malcolm left.

He not only left, but he took the rent money with him. When I called and asked him to drop it off, he simply told me he was going to use the money to move into a new place. He also told me he didn't care if they put my daughter and me out of the house. In his mind, we could be homeless or go back to Albany. I couldn't believe it, after ten years of friendship.

I knew that our friendship was over.

I felt like I had lost my friend, my dignity, and I thought I would lose my apartment too, but God was with me through all of this.

WHEN GOD LET ME SPEAK~175

Things got pretty hard for Flo and me. His car

broke down, causing him to take a leave of absence from his job. About a week later, I finally got a job making $15 an hour versus the $12 that I was making with Williams-Sonoma.

I had to work my rent out with my leasing company for months while I waited to start my new position. I don't think things have ever been this hard. Flo and I were obviously to-gether now and living together.

We not only had to keep our heads above water but learn each other and how to be together, as well.

The lights and internet were in Darren's name, and within the next few weeks, he cut them off one by one. That left us with reconnection costs and lost time from work.

We had to live with the lights off for two days.

The thing is, though, God has never let us down. Our

neighbors brought us food and allowed us to run lights from their house to ours. Without power, we were still in the house, eating, watching TV, and living.

176~LISAMARIE THOMAS

Then came the eviction.

The apartment complex tried to send an eviction about three months later, but God intervened again. They were trying to cover their ass by helping me but still evicting me for non-payment at the same time.

Whoever sent the eviction notice to DeKalb County Courthouse made a spelling error. They spelled Parkway wrong by spelling it Parkwy. The sheriff came to serve the eviction but could not serve it because of the error.

About two weeks later, Flo and I had paid the deposit on a two-bedroom townhome in College Park. We had all the utilities cut on and moved in the following week.

We moved in on October 1, 2019, but 2020 was just around the corner and this crazy ass turn of events, was nowhere finished with us yet.

WHEN GOD LET ME SPEAK~177

1. X

Justified Insecurity

What does it mean when a person's insecurities are validated?

We justify their actions, the things that they say to us, and the way they treat us. This happens when someone that we love is going through something or has recently gone through a traumatic experience.

We feel we understand this person needs time to get over what has happened, and we know that in that time, this person may act differently than they normally would.

178

WHEN GOD LET ME SPEAK~179

What happens when this person is close to you, like a spouse, mother, father, child, or a best friend?

Do we give ourselves a time limit for how long we continue to deal with their grieving period?

XXI

Renegade

I've always struggled with depression.

In my mind, my life was a wheel of tragedy, and I was always going to end up on the bottom.

Life has been a battle of me constantly losing myself. Every time I thought I knew who I was, every time I felt stronger, something would come my way to break me back down.

Every time, the fall gets harder.

I used to be at a point where I felt like nothing could hold me back.

180

WHEN GOD LET ME SPEAK~181

There have been more times than now that I've just accepted defeat.

I'm becoming content with what my life offers me, even if it's nothing good. Don't start looking at me like that; I'm looking at it this way.

At least, I can keep my sanity instead of believing that one day, things will be different for me.

This is a renegade chapter.

It is a chapter of rediscovery through self-analysis. It's not a complete analysis by far, but I needed a foundation to start.

Some people would associate the term renegade with disloyalty. However, the best definition for the word is simply making a different choice. Too often, society generalizes following the crowd as being loyal. What happens when we all fail at life because we were never loyal to ourselves.

I haven't been loyal to myself.

You can't imagine how many people close to me couldn't see how that was a problem.

182~LISAMARIE THOMAS

That didn't hurt until I realized it was a problem myself. I looked around me and felt like I was in a box. I couldn't trust anybody around me.

I've always been a loner, but for a long time, I didn't really want to be. I wanted to be a social butterfly. I wanted to be one of the popular girls.

At first, I wanted to be the girl that all the boys wanted.

Honestly, contrary to what you're thinking, I'm sure... Here's some clarification.

I didn't want to be a thot.

I just wanted to be known.

I wanted to feel like somebody.

I also knew that there were attributing factors to success,

and I felt I needed to have those. I'm even discovering, as I write this, how long I have been truly searching for a purpose and a place in this world.

I've had people tell me I wasn't smart enough, good enough, or pretty enough.

WHEN GOD LET ME SPEAK~183

I'm constantly trying to convince myself that I'm worth more than what everyone says I am.

I'm constantly trying to differ from everyone who has convinced themselves that I am. That has been one of the hardest things to admit to myself.

There are so many times that I felt I should die.

I sat there and held back tears, as they told me I was only smart in computers and nothing else. From the mouth of someone I loved, I carried the worst pain in my heart.

I couldn't believe that when the people that you love said things to hurt you, it would scar you.

It was crazy because I could believe nothing negative from someone that didn't know me.

However, harsh words have a bigger impact when it comes from someone that has watched them help other people.

Someone that has watched them overcome tragedy or struggle to take care of their children alone; or someone that has seen them starve and watched their best attempts to be strong.

184~LISAMARIE THOMAS

How am I ever supposed to trust anyone?

How am I supposed to fall in love and get married?

Hell, how am I supposed to be happy?

This was when I decided I could truly be content alone. All alone. Just me and my children and no one else.

I could listen to Ariana Grande, Billie Eilish, Dax or Hopsin and be completely content. I would be happy with my daughter for life, and smoke weed on the back porch of my mansion in California.

I made a conscious decision to deter from following everyone else, helping everyone else, doing for everyone else. I stopped taking everyone's feelings and circumstances into consideration all the time.

I stopped doing for everyone else what I couldn't do for myself. I would not do it for people that would devalue my self-worth.

WHEN GOD LET ME SPEAK~185

I had finally decided how unfair that was to me.

That's when I understood the true meaning of loyalty.

I understood it started with me, and without loyalty to myself, I would always be disloyal. Now, it matters less what everyone else thinks, including my closest loved ones.

That might not sound the best, and if you're one, that's reading this.

Well, I'm sorry.

No, I'm just kidding.

Don't close the book.

Understand that this means that I care more about what I think now. I care more about what I believe about myself. I care more about what I know is true about myself and my character.

I believe it is most important to stay close to the good in me.

I realize now that if anyone hurts me by their actions or the words that they speak, whether intentionally or unintentionally, I should listen.

186~LISAMARIE THOMAS

There are so many times that I am caught up in anger, and I constantly miss if God is trying to tell me something or point me in the right direction.

I know God is calculated. He sends messages out appropriately, even if it sounds horrible.

I don't say any of these things because I believe everything or even the negative that is spoken up on me, but because I want to pull any message that will strengthen me, be more focused or more determined.

I used the negativity as fuel, and here I am again, writing at 3:12 in the morning.

Aside from going through traumatic experiences, I've thought about taking my life because I didn't like who I was. I believed that my life was unfair.

I know that sounds completely selfish, but I just couldn't understand why so many events that could affect my psychological well-being would happen to me.

Why did they have to happen constantly?

WHEN GOD LET ME SPEAK~187

I can't count the number of times that I've wondered what a "normal life" was?

What did growing up in a "normal family" feel like?

The regret that I consistently felt put a "Butterfly Effect" vibe on me.

Many nights that I lay in my bed, staring off into space

with thoughts of changing different parts of my life, I wondered if it was possible and what would happen if I did.

I wondered, would my life be better or worse? Would I lose someone important to me, or would I lose my life earlier than I would have?

I didn't realize how hard it would be to ride the wave of life without knowing where the fuck you're going.

There's one more important part that I just realized.

No matter how hard the wave or how fast the wave is, the easiest person to guide the steering wheel is me.

I'm controlling my boat, so why would I listen to passengers on the boat telling me where to go?

188~LISAMARIE THOMAS

If I'm steering my plane, why would I listen to the flight attendants telling me how fast to go or how to handle the turbulence?

When I look at it from that perspective, it seems so simple, and I kind of feel stupid.

Then again, that's the behavior that I'm trying to stop.

So yes, I changed allegiance from everyone else to myself. If you call that treacherous, then I feel sorry for how you treat yourself.

I would not fall into a depression anymore because of the way someone feels about me.

I can't give up my life because I believed I was nothing, that I was worthless, that I didn't have any goals, that I was lazy, that I was a bad parent, that I was stupid, that I deserved the things that happened to me.

No, because I wasn't any of that. I didn't feel that it was fair that I had to defend my character, but then I realized I don't need to.

WHEN GOD LET ME SPEAK~189

My conscience is clear when I have admitted and apologized for my wrong-doings and when I do my best to not make the same mistakes.

My conscience is clear when I still think of others' needs and care for them, regardless of the way they have treated me.

My conscience is clear when I have good intentions and attempt to do things a little better every day.

Now, I'm deciding that my life is worth thinking of myself first. My kids are worth thinking about and believing in myself first.

Not second, and surely not last.

I deserved to love myself and make myself happy, and I couldn't let even the closest person take that away.

I couldn't let someone who lay next to me every night convince me I wasn't worth that.

At that point, I would truly become nothing, and I feel like I'm a little stronger than that.

I decided that whatever I needed to do to get to the point of happiness and not defeat, I would do it.

XXII

Selfish

I got to a point in my life that after all the damage I had taken, I became closed off. I wanted people to know less about me; I wanted fewer friends; I even wanted to be seen less.

It wasn't because I didn't feel attractive now; it was because I felt like everyone could see my pain. I felt like I wore it, like a sign, and I was honestly ashamed of that.

The surrounding people didn't seem to have as many problems as me, and the last thing I wanted to feel like was a burden on anyone, even emotionally.

190

WHEN GOD LET ME SPEAK~191

I wanted to appear normal, as if I didn't walk around with so much fear and doubt.

The scars were hard to hide, though, and it wasn't as easy as I thought it would be to disappear from the actual world. The further I went into life, the more I felt like people didn't understand me. I wondered why I should even bother letting people in. It would hurt me more to take on assumptions and judgment. It seemed smarter to fight those battles alone.

I had determined over the years that my thoughts or opinions didn't matter. I felt that every situation that I got into would take more of my life from me because I was giving it to someone else.

Eventually, I would end up drowning, trying to save everyone else.

I knew then that it was more important that I saved myself.

I sat back and thought about it.

I had spent five years with someone.

192~LISAMARIE THOMAS

I spent years helping him live, helping him

get through school, and try to give him things that he wanted in a woman. I never thought about myself.

I have plenty of skills, but I was using them to develop everyone else except myself.

I was basically sleeping on myself. I'm not gonna lie; there are a lot of times that I regret the lost time. I mean, can you blame me?

I have enough sense to know that everything happens for a reason, but I'm human too.

Now that I have had a lot of time to think about it, I never know how I really feel. I honestly feel like I may never know until I can see the light at the end of the tunnel.

If the end goal was within reach, somehow, I think I would gain clarity.

After I moved back from Atlanta, my mindset had changed dramatically, but I wasn't exactly where I needed to be.

Yes, I had learned caution, logic, and many other life lessons, but I hadn't learned quite how to love myself yet.

WHEN GOD LET ME SPEAK~193

I think this situation might have taught me everything that I needed to know.

I dated this guy for a while after I moved back to Albany. We met in a neighborhood Walmart, and he seemed… well… normal. He was a cashier, dark-skinned with a pretty white smile. His name was D. He was a year older than me, and I thought that might have been a pleasant change because all of my failed relationships and situationships were with guys that were five and six years older than me.

It made sense that if I dated someone on my age level,

even if I was a little more mature as a female, there would be more common ground and room for growth.

I had spent too much time feeling invalidated and treated like the demons in my head weren't there. Everyone needed someone to lean on, and I was tired of being that person.

D was sweet, and I needed that. He looked exactly like the emotional support that I was looking for.

194~LISAMARIE THOMAS

I don't know what you're thinking right now, but we're probably on the same page. This whole thought process was stupid. You would have thought I would have learned already.

I thought five months would have been enough time to return to normal, but here I was again. Riding the wave that would keep me from drowning.

I loved how sweet he was to me. We would text all throughout the day, and he would even drive to my job on my breaks, even if it was only a few minutes. He did a lot to show me he was a good person and had my best interest.

In all honesty, he may have, if I had been ready to be involved with someone else, but I wasn't. I had allowed how he made me feel to determine where my life focus was going to be, and I messed up, yet again.

It took a lot less time for me to see that D was just like the others. He wasted no time capitalizing on the fact that I would give my all to him and that I did my best to be a good person. I wouldn't even call him a manipulator for doing that; he was more of an opportunist.

WHEN GOD LET ME SPEAK~195

When I could make him glad, everything was fine, but

the moment things got rough for us or even in his personal life, he used me to deflect. It started with him saying hurtful things, then it graduated to him lying about everything, even to his family.

When we moved in together, he had some trouble finding a job, and I got a work-from-home position. Everything was going well because we had enough to pay the bills and maintain. I understood he was a man, and me handling things took a toll on his ego, but it wasn't worth what he did.

To make a long story short, the house was owned by his parents. All the money we gave them for bills, he would tell them he made. He made it seem like he was working and I wasn't. So, my child and I were just lying up under him while he did all the work.

196~LISAMARIE THOMAS

To his mom, I was just a lazy female, taking advantage of her son. In fact, it may have been just the opposite.

I didn't notice something might have been wrong until his mother's disposition with me changed. That made me ask questions, and it took him almost three months to tell me the truth.

In all honesty, it fucked me up in the head. It wasn't him, personally. It was the fact that I had allowed someone in, and they took advantage of me again.

I blamed myself, and that was pretty difficult, but I also realized that it was a step forward for me, personally. I had finally acknowledged one thing that I was doing wrong in my life, and that was the first step to recovery in any situation.

At this point in my life, if I didn't take some responsibility for the situations that I ended up in, I could never change my life.

You might as well call me an idiot, and I definitely did not want to be that.

The next step that I took in my personal journey was to make the future about my children and me.

WHEN GOD LET ME SPEAK~197

After D, I was completely overgiving myself to anyone else. It wasn't even worth it. Neither I nor my children benefited from any situation at one time, and it took a long time for me to realize how unfair that was.

Once I got to that point, it seemed like everyone else changed too. They had to notice that I wasn't giving anymore.

I started not to care about things that didn't concern me as much. That made me seem inconsiderate. I spoke my mind more, then I looked like a bitch to everyone.

It kind of hurt that everyone could be selfish, but they thought that I shouldn't. It hurt me that people could constantly hurt me, but I was told to be humble.

In my mind, everyone that hurt me didn't feel the pain that I did.

That made me feel like people either didn't understand me or just didn't care at all.

My trust became completely fucked up then,

as if it wasn't already.

198~LISAMARIE THOMAS

For a while, I wallowed in a deep depression. Not only did I blame myself, but I also became content bottling up the rage, pain, betrayal, heartbreak, guilt, and the many other demons living in my head.

I didn't know how to get away from them,

so I let it consume me.

When I did that, the rest of my life fell apart, and I had allowed that. I became inoperable.

I thanked God every day that my best friend was there for me, at that point in my life.

I got so low that I couldn't even care for my daughter for weeks.

My daughter and I were in the same house, but I would sleep for hours, sometimes almost a full day. I walked around with tears in my eyes.

I couldn't hold my head up, and when I did, I had to laugh to keep from crying.

I had almost given up on myself. It was one thing that I allowed everyone else to break me, but it was major when I broke myself.

WHEN GOD LET ME SPEAK~199

One day, though, I came out of it.

I didn't want to hurt anymore.

I wanted to live up to my full potential, and that meant living for me.

Out of nowhere, I had to pick myself up.

I couldn't allow myself to die out so that my daughter could live the same life as me or even go through the same tragedy.

That meant I had to finish the race. I had to do it, regardless of what anyone thought of me and regardless of how I felt.

My journey was so much larger than me.

If that meant I would have to be selfish to save the lives of me and my children, so be it.

Call me selfish.

XXIII

Diary of an Introverted

Intuitive

I first started to question if I was happy, when I felt like my identity was being lost.

At the point that I didn't know who I was, it was piercing. It was kind of tormenting too because identity is a terrible thing to waste.

I can't really remember when I first felt that way, but it had to be when I was around twenty.

Ever since then, I've been searching to figure out what would fill the void that I have in my heart.

200

WHEN GOD LET ME SPEAK~201

I had become content with whom I was. Happy, even. Most would say that's a bad thing, but I would beg to differ with survival.

There have been days where I just lay in the bed and cried because I had everything that I could want in my life, but there was still this sadness.

There was always a deep sad-ness surrounding me, and I

couldn't fight it. I couldn't run from it, and I couldn't escape it. It was deafening.

Piercing sounds of nothing fill my ears on dark days. When the people I love would reach out, I could only shut them down.

The unidentified pain in my soul keeps me from feeling anything sometimes, and that's what scares me the most.

The inability to feel or to connect with others was against my will, but to my brain, it was necessary. To block out the pain.

Eventually, I knew I had to change something in order for me to be okay.

I had to learn how to work through a bunch of issues that I didn't even know I had.

202~LISAMARIE THOMAS

For years, I felt like I didn't have to work through anything. None of my issues were bothering anybody. What difference would it make if I continued to close myself off from everybody?

From my perspective then, my loved ones would just have to accept who I was. I wasn't immoral, disloyal, or anything of the like. In fact, most would say I was the exact opposite, but they would most likely follow up with, "She's a certified bitch."

Could anybody really believe that I didn't want to be this way?

Is it that hard to believe that I don't want to feel angry, negative, and coarse?

In all honesty, I want to trust people far more than I do, but I just can't. I just can't.

Stay away from everybody; that's what I convinced myself to do. That hurt more than you think.

I acted like I didn't feel it, but being lonely is pretty low.

For anybody.

WHEN GOD LET ME SPEAK~203

More and more soul-searching turned up no results. It had become incredibly frustrating that I couldn't figure out who I was.

Let me be the one to tell you.

It is incredibly hard to be living in a person who you don't understand. The thing is, the purpose that is driving me is constantly conflicting with the person who is inside of me.

These two capacities share the same values, ambitions, and character, but they could never run properly.

I've never reached my full potential.

I know it's there. From fighting my demons to figuring them out, I keep praying that there is an endgame. I needed it badly.

This lack of marriage between my two worlds caused me to see my gifts as a curse.

How do you speak up to yourself? How do you reclaim your mentality after your own hand has lost it?

I gotta figure out how to stop fucking up my life so that I can help someone else.

204~LISAMARIE THOMAS

XXIV

Fear of Dying

You probably think these stories are depressing as hell, right?

Me, too, but who else could I tell them to?

You're listening, aren't you?

Well, reading it anyway.

These stories, reflections, and experiences changed everything about me, but I couldn't escape this constant fear of dying.

The constant dream that I would have of death was giving the most fucked up vision of my future.

205

206~LISAMARIE THOMAS

What if I took every dream, vision, and nightmare as a warning of spiritual death?

What if it is the coming of spiritual growth?

What if this was a dream of lost purpose and self?

I decided I had to continue building up everything that I had lost.

What if I took all the pain and applied it to building another woman up or helping another woman grow?

What if I could convert the tragedy and suffering into a social platform that could benefit millions of women?

What if I could change the lives of other women by the simple realization that there is someone out there like them who knows the magnitude of what they're going through?

Maybe I could find comfort in knowing that there is someone out there, just like me.

What if I could make it possible that women were not as afraid to speak up anymore?

WHEN GOD LET ME SPEAK~207

What if they weren't as afraid to be who they were anymore? I wanted to create a change from this that gave more women free will and the ability to empathize with each other.

I wanted to give other women the chance to share their stories, as well. I thought about a healing chain of people. Leaning more towards compassion and understanding for one another.

A social world that exemplified tolerance, teaching, and peace.

Maybe we can bridge some of the social and stereotypical gaps that have been the foundation of the destruction of relationships, families, friendships, and homes.

If I can create a catalyst for this type of movement, it would challenge the standard way of thinking, reverse the desensitization and hate displayed between women and my race of people.

I have to try to recreate social norms, so we all have the chance to exceed our potential. Maybe all of this wasn't for nothing.

Then comes the "AHA" MOMENT, finally.

I went through all of this for a reason.

208~LISAMARIE THOMAS

You're probably reading this and thinking, "DUH," RIGHT?

Look, this journey was much harder than you think?

Cut me a little slack. We all go through stuff.

I'll be damned if this life came with a manual because I would have been Beyonce or LeBron James by now.

I had to go through the emotions, too, to figure out how I was going to contribute to the world because I knew I had to.

Now I'm thinking that my purpose could be to create a better world, starting with the women that have been torn down as I have.

Then we could branch out to our communities and our men, especially our black men, who have been destroyed in the same way?

At that point, we can start rebuilding what our oppressors have stolen from us.

I need all of that back.

We need all of that back, especially my black and brown women.

WHEN GOD LET ME SPEAK~209

Our individuality, understanding of who we are, and capacity to understand and grow with one another instead of against one another.

Some situations have taken our ability to trust, love, and believe in each other.

At one point, that was all we had. Women, at one point, we were all we had.

Now, we can't look at each other without hate and envy while our own black men and everyone from outside races are plotting to bring us down, as well.

We get sex trafficked, abused, raped, beaten, degraded, sexualized, and belittled. There has to be a point where we realize we can only save ourselves.

Someone has to help start a new movement.

That's what I will stand for.

I think that I have found my purpose.

Afterword

IT HAS BEEN A PLEASURE SHARING MY EXPERI-ENCES WITH YOU.

THIS NOVEL IS ONE THAT HAS PUSHED ME FOR-WARD IN MY OWN LIFE WHEN I

THOUGHT ABOUT GIVING UP, AND I HOPE THAT IT WILL DO THE SAME FOR SOMEONE ELSE.

KEEP GOD IN EVERYTHING THAT YOU DO

&

REMEMBER

211

212~Afterword

WE LIVE BY LEARNED BEHAVIOR, EXPERIENCE, AND KNOWLEDGE.

MASTERING PERCEPTION IN LIFE LEADS US DOWN THE PATH OF TRUE

SELF-KNOWLEDGE, ACCEPTANCE, AND UNDER-STANDING.

LISA MARIE THOMAS

Acknowledgments & Thank You's

I've enjoyed you all so much! This has officially been a roller coaster right?

Let me first Thank God, for guiding me every step along the way.

To My Family & Friends:

Thank you to my mom, Lisa Lajuan Coates for paving the way for me. You have been my mentor, mother, and friend and it is your journey and resilience that showed me how to be strong.

I realize that more than ever now.

More than I did at the end of my first book.

My understanding has advanced so much more since then. You helped transform me into a woman and mother without even knowing it and I thank you every day for that.

Thank you Mommy Lorraine, from the bottom of my heart for being my mother at the time that my mother could not and at the time in my life, that I needed you the most. You instilled in me the character and morals and values that I needed to be the person that I am today.

Ms. Teressa,

you may be new in my life but you came into my life at a time that I needed to be close to my mom and you stepped in and became a mentor and mother figure for me,

at a time in my life when I needed help with becoming a better mother, woman, and wife.

My Sister & Brother From Another Mother

Michelle and Maurice - Thank You for always being there for me.

I love you guys to death.

My baby brother Stephon and my brothers Raimundo & both Julians

(Yes, I have 2 actual brothers with the same name.)

My fiance, Kokaine Flo;

for supporting me throughout this whole journey, even in the times that I thought I was alone. I thank God for you every day, and you don't even know it.

My children for firing up my ambition.

I even thank my ex-friends and my haters even, you'll get love too for being the motivation that I needed to run my black ass straight out of the hood.

For My Readers:

I'm sincerely hoping that somebody,

somewhere took something from this story

that might make them a better person.

We could all benefit from being better in some way,

You Can't Deny It!

Even You,

Sitting there like you can!

Forget the Fear,

Doubt and Self-Pity!

Don't let anyone stop you

from achieving your purpose

or reaching your dreams.

It is your birthright to be the best motherfucking you that you

can be!

Never forget that!

Never let anyone tell you different

You're not what anyone says you are

I promise you that!

Not your family, friends, teachers, colleagues or even your spouse.

It's not true!

Push past your boundaries and your fears.

Realize who you are, and what God put you here for.

As a Final Word of Advice:

Work Your Ass Off

Don't Look Crazy because it's not that hard!

Just get up and do it.

The energy that you spend every day entertaining fake friends,

social media, habits, and opinions.

Put all that energy into yourself and your internal happiness.

You won't regret it!

Preserve your personal peace because it's yours and Never Allow Anyone to take that away from you!

Can you promise me that?

Always remember,

That Faith without work is dead

That means, put your faith in God first

Start Changing Your Life Next,

&

Get your money, boo

It's Our Time Now!

Thank You Again to My Readers

Additional Thanks to my audiobook narrators

Lianna, Michelle Dozier, and Kokaine Flo.

This meant the world to me.

If you haven't read my first book,
Turned Out.
Well, you should!
It is available on Amazon.com
and many other online retailers and local bookstores.

Partners & Sponsors

PGDK Entertainment LLC
SVN 10 Gourmet Wing & Fries Eatery LLC - Atlanta, Ga
Lisamarie Thomas Publishing LLC
Mattress Fast LLC - Atlanta, Ga
Extend-A-Brush Inc.
Also check out new music by
Kokaine Flo Tha Great,
New Mixtape available on all music platforms by the end
of the year!
I'll Let Him Give Ya'll the Name of It
@ www.everybodyhateskokaineflo.com
and Don't Forget to Drop a 5 Star Review
Free My Baby Brother Lil 9ine
New Mixtape Coming Soon
Stay Up Lil Bro

This one's for you...

About the Author

After turning 18, Lisamarie tried chasing her dreams, taking the first step of moving to the big city of Atlanta, Ga.

In 2017, after surviving human trafficking; she made a conscious decision to stop making mistakes and start understanding her situation.

Realizing, she had to confront the darkness inside of her to reach the light.

She seemed to discover her purpose.

In 2020, she released her Best-Selling Autobiography: Turned Out, documenting her escape from her abuser.

Shortly after in 2021, she released the novella, When God Let Me Speak.

In a unique way, Lisamarie attempts to understand and heal her pain by analyzing the things that have taken place in her life, so far.

Through short stories, she focuses on finding out who you truly are within, reversing cycles of negativity in your life, and growing up physically, mentally, emotionally, and spiritually.

Most recently, she authored her first children's book, along with her daughter Lianna Michelle Dozier.

The book is titled: Don't Call Me Pretty.

Focusing on understanding cultural vanity; in a way that is inspirational and entertaining.

The primary purpose of this book is to help children understand that morality, skills, values and the core traits that create a person are the most important part of who you are.

In this story, the main character Leah is great, in all things.

Even though she shows greatness in every part of her life, she still feels insecure and under-appreciated by her friends.

She shows great determination to be more than just a pretty face.

"Understanding that every child may not show an A+ in every subject or win first place in every contest.

The goal is to start the conversation on a subject that holds major weight in our society.

As social activists, we want to not only help heal adults but save the lives of our children. This is just as important.

It is my belief that having a positive effect on children could act as a preventative therapy, so our children don't continue to fall in the same holes that their previous generation has. " - Lisamarie Thomas

These books have become best-sellers on Amazon.

Her upcoming release IMPRISONED: An Anthology, is another type of short story novel, written by herself and several authors.

Our lives have become a box that we cannot get out of.

Confined to our own little personal prisons, but why?

Is it fear?

Conditioning?

Challenging the standard way of thinking;

Dare You To Try?

Will You Break Free?

Follow on IG @LisamarieTheAuthor